DANSE MACABRE

THE NEVE & EGAN CASES, BOOK 3

CRISTELLE COMBY

ALSO BY CRISTELLE COMBY

The Neve & Egan Cases

RUSSIAN DOLLS

RUBY HEART

DANSE MACABRE

BLIND CHESS

Vale Investigation

HOSTILE TAKEOVER

EVIL EMBERS

AVENGING SPIRIT

GHOST SHIP

TIME AGAIN

Stand Alone Stories

RED LIES

ALONE TOGETHER

ALSO BY CRISTELLE COMBY

Short Stories

Personal Favour (*Neve & Egan* prequel)

Redemption Road (*Vale Investigation* prequel)

The short stories are exclusively available on the author's website:

www.cristelle-comby.com/freebooks

CONTENTS

Cover by: Arté Digital Graphics

Edition: 1

ISBN: 1502723778
ISBN-13: 978-1502723772

PROLOGUE

I have never played chess before, but I seem to have found myself in the midst of a deadly game against a skilled adversary. I reckon I better learn the rules... and quickly.

"Chess: The King's Game. Successful players must demonstrate skill in strategy, tactics, and foresight. The aim is to kill your opponent's king before he has the opportunity to kill yours..." Or at least that's what it says in the second-hand book I just bought from Camden Market.

I became an unwitting pawn in a life-size game about a year ago. It feels like a lifetime ago now. So much has changed since then; I have changed. Now if somebody asks me what I do for a living, my answer is private investigator — no pause, no hesitation.

Last year I was a university student, dividing my time between history and literature lectures, when my best friend, Irina Anderson, was murdered. She was nothing but collateral damage in the war against organised crime being fought on the streets of London, the innocent daughter of a fraudster in league with the Russian Mafia. She was a small, unwitting cog in a well-oiled machine manufactured by one man — London's most wanted man — the puppet master who pulls all the strings from his secure place, hidden in the shadows. A man known only by his alias, a nickname, whispered by those in the know: The Sorter.

For the right price, he can sort anything. He has his fingers in pies, so to speak. If you want weapons, drugs, prostitutes, games rigged, or if you need to end a life prematurely, he is the man to call.

I've never met him. I don't know his real identity. To me he is just a shadow. I wish I could say it goes both ways, but he knows me and he my business partner, Ashford Egan, by names.

Egan and I opened our private investigation agency after closing that first case. The same day as I posted my affiliation request to the Association of British Investigators, I got my first "gift" from the Sorter. An unsealed enveloped, left on the floor outside my flat. Among other things, it contained a chess piece, a black pawn.

The next time one of our investigations put us in the Sorter's way, Egan and I received a second envelope. A black bishop that time and another eerie handwritten note which read, 'Until next time.' It thoroughly chilled me, even though it was a sunny afternoon, and the temperature was well above average.

Deep down, I know the Sorter could crush us in an instant if he so desired. He has the resources to ensure our bodies would never be found. I guess we must be a source of amusement for him.

'Are we playing a game?' Egan had asked me after we received the second chess piece.

'Yes,' I'd told him. 'Whether we want to or not — it seems we do not have the choice.' And so, I decided it was time I learned to play.

With tensed shoulders, I lower the book in my hand. Massaging the tight spot between my shoulder blades, I chance a look outside my bedroom window. Snow is still falling — cottony pearls coming down in intervals.

Although it's only the last week of November, the weather has been as bleak as can be for London. Every day this past week has seen a thin layer of snow cover the ground. Today, the clouds seem bottomless, and with no winds to alter their course, flakes fall in straight lines, one after the other.

I lean forward for a better look at Camden Street below, and find that the snow reaches the first step of the little phone shop under my flat. A chill courses the length of my arms at the sight, and I snuggle more deeply into the afghan wrapped around my shoulders.

'Will it ever stop?' I mutter at the window with frost settling in its corners. I hate winters. It makes travelling around town even more difficult than usual. London's Underground is not all that efficient at the best of times, let alone with huge amounts of snow on the lines. Yet, there isn't much of an alternative — I don't want to think about what it must be like to try to take a car out in this white hell.

I'm glad the *Neve & Egan - Private Eyes Agency*'s latest case, which was on the other side of town, was wrapped up two days ago. Our investigation took place in a fancy casino on the south bank of London — some croupier had found a way to rig the roulette table. His boss should have paid more attention to his CV when he hired him; then maybe he would have been suspicious as to why an engineer with a doctorate suddenly yearned for a career change. Egan and I had to cross town every day while we were on the case, and it was a tough one to crack, what with neither of us being particularly technology-minded.

This was our — I scrunch my brow in thought — twenty-fourth case. The casino's owner promised to refer people our way if he ever got the chance, and he tipped us kindly. I smile at the thought, remembering how money was so hard to come by when we first started.

We launched our agency with nothing in the bank. For the first few months, Egan continued working part-time as a university professor to make ends meet. All we had, to begin with were a few business cards, an ad in the Yellow Pages that read "Private Investigators providing comprehensive, all-round services. We diligently seek out the truth for our clients. Discretion assured" and a lot of goodwill. From day one, we knew word of mouth would be the only way to succeed.

Two of our latest clients were referred to us by previous customers, and a friend in the Metropolitan Police sends people our way sometimes when the system can't help. Of course, we still get the occasional lost dog to search for, but the future is looking brighter. Cases have become more interesting, our rainy day account is healthier, and Egan and I even talked the other day about having our own office. Sure, we would need to find a real bargain, but it's on next year's agenda.

Noticing the time, I slip a bookmark into my chess manual and uncurl my long legs from the settee. Moving to the mirror in my bedroom, I gather my dark hair and braid it into a plait which then rests on my right shoulder. Slipping into some faux-fur snow boots, I spare one languid look at my beloved, but for now redundant, Converse trainers. With a sigh again at the weather, I shrug my shoulders into my duffle coat and grab my gloves and hat.

The cold that hits me as I push open the front door is almost enough to make me scurry back inside. I push my gloved hands deep into my coat pockets and hurry down to the Underground station.

Some two hours later, I arrive at my friend's flat, having cursed the snow, London Transport and life in general in English, Italian and something which may or may not have been grammatically correct German.

My friend and business partner, Ashford Egan, lives in a cosy flat on the first floor of a two-storey, red-brick house on Herbrand Street, not too far from University College London where he used to teach. His quiet street is covered with a thick layer of snow that is unbroken save for a few footprints here and there. The lampposts are the only way to tell where the pavement ends and the road begins.

I find no visible footprints by Egan's building as I climb the steps. I almost drop the heavy shoulder bag I'm carrying as I try to open the wooden door one-handed. I try my best to leave the snow from my boots on the doormat before taking the stairs up. On the first floor, I knock four times at my friend's door — in my trademark rhythmic sequence, to let him know it's me — and he opens shortly afterwards.

'*Buongiorno Signore,*' I greet him in Italian, my father's native language.

Egan offers me a smile and a polite bow of his head. I fleetingly note that his hair needs a cut. It's the longest I've ever seen it, and the ginger curls that I always suspected existed are starting to show.

I leave my snow boots in the hall and enter the warmth of his flat with a relieved smile.

'As much as your visit pleases me, I wasn't expecting to see you today,' Egan says, as he closes the front door.

I walk down the long, bare corridor that leads to the living room, flick the light switch on and turn straight to the right to enter the open kitchen.

'A promise is a promise,' I reply, dropping the grocery bag on the glass top of his kitchen table. I take off my coat and place it on the back of a nearby chair with the rest of my winter gear.

'How bad is it?' He enters the kitchen, leans himself against the low white wall that separates the kitchen from the living room. 'They said several inches on the radio.'

'About ten inches now,' I reply, 'and it keeps piling up and up.'

Egan rubs at the bridge of his nose and lets out a long, martyred sigh.

I feel bad for him. For a blind person, walking around in snow can be more than a little hazardous, and my friend avoids it as much as possible. I know he isn't the most outdoorsy person in the world, quite the contrary, but being forced to stay inside is eating him up. I suppose what he finds enraging is not having the choice. How rude it is of the seasonal weather to force his hand.

I could offer to accompany him outside, but I doubt he would appreciate the gesture. I discovered when I befriended Egan that there is little he values more than his independence.

He does not take kindly to me trying to 'mother-hen' him, as he says, so I've learned to refrain from the urge.

'I got everything from your list,' I say, as I start to unpack the groceries. 'Except the *fraises des bois*.'

With a serious face, he raises an elegant querying eyebrow, above blue eyes aimed a little to my left.

'Seriously, Ash, where in the hell was I supposed to find fresh wild strawberries in the middle of an Ice Age?'

The seriousness on his face lingers for a couple of seconds before a grin breaks, letting me know the odd request had been a joke all along. I chuckle at the jest, and he walks forward.

He feels along the surface of the table until he finds the first of the groceries: a milk bottle. He holds it with both hands, nods, and goes to place it inside the fridge. He returns to the table and does the same with every other item I bought.

I let him be and move to the living room where I slump down on his over-comfortable leather settee, with a contented sigh. For once, I am glad that Egan's thick curtains hide his windows and the snow that continues to fall outside.

'Dare I enquire about your "Friday night out?"' my friend asks from the kitchen.

Damn it! I curse, inwardly. From the moment I let it slip that I had a date planned, I knew I would come to regret it.

'Nothing to say,' I grumble. 'Matthew cancelled.' I let the *again* be unsaid, but it's plain to hear in my tone.

'Again?' Egan asks, and I groan in frustration.

Matthew Stenson is a detective sergeant in London's Metropolitan Police Force. He investigates murders at New Scotland Yard. We first met in February, when his division investigated Irina's death. He helped us solve the case — or maybe it was the other way around. We worked together again a couple of months later, when a stolen necklace case turned into a home invasion, with a side of assault and battery, topped with a murder investigation.

There had been a spark of *something* between Stenson and me since the beginning, and it got more serious over the summer. Well, it would have, if only we could manage to spend some time together. In truth, we've had two complete dates, four aborted dates, and six cancelled dates. I know I shouldn't be counting, but I can't help it. Last night could have been *the* night, but the body of a young woman found in East London two days ago thwarted our plans. As frustrating as the situation is, I can hardly blame Stenson for it, having had to cancel myself, twice, because of work.

'Maybe we're not meant for each other after all,' I half-whisper, half-moan from my slumped position on the settee.

'Nonsense,' Egan says from the kitchen, having heard me as clearly as if I'd been standing right next to him. 'You two will get it on wonderfully.'

A while ago, a phrase like that would have made me blush. I'm pleased to note that I am getting used to Egan's odd innuendos.

My partner, who has the social interaction level of a monk taking a vow of silence, decided somewhere along the way that Stenson and I are meant for each other. Since then, he's taken to dropping not so subtle hints and insinuation at every possible opportunity.

I don't rise to the bait, and say, 'Not before they've caught whoever killed young Carlie Egger, I'm afraid.' Hopefully, this titbit will suffice to redirect the conversation away from my personal life. 'Heard about it?'

Egan hums from the kitchen. 'Yes, it made the radio news this morning. Eighteen and an accomplished professional pianist, wasn't she? Looked as though she was well on her way to becoming a soloist for the Royal Philharmonic Orchestra. Such a shame; they perform wonderful renditions of classical masterpieces.'

I knew all of that, and shiver as I recall Stenson's grave tone on the phone as he explained why he had to cancel. 'Matt told me the murder was grisly. Carlie had been missing for about two weeks, before they found her in an abandoned warehouse transformed into some kind of a mock-up concert hall, with a stage and a grand piano.'

'Quite a gruesome way to die, indeed,' my friend says, walking past the settee with a cup of tea in each hand. He holds one out in my general direction.

'Thanks,' I mutter, reaching for the cup and taking a sip.

Egan sits down in a chair, to my right. 'Do they have any leads?'

'Nothing so far, so they're all putting in the extra hours. The story made the front page of *The Sun,* and their orders are to find the killer *presto.'*

Egan remains silent; my love life is forgotten.

'I hope they find the bastard who did it.'

1

The snow stopped falling four days ago, but I hear there's little to rejoice about. According to meteorologists, it will start falling again soon; today's only the fifth of December after all, and winter is far from over. For the time being, the hard work of the City's gritters, coupled with some feeble rays of sun, cleared most of London's roads. There is still the odd patch of ice to be mindful of when walking through the streets, but life has resumed its usual frantic pace.

Donning a long navy-blue woollen scarf and hat, I meet with Egan in St. Pancras. My friend is wearing a thick dark overcoat and a scarf of his own. No hat, though; his ginger curls undulate in the wind. He folds his white cane as I approach, and I offer him my arm to hold onto, as we walk to the Tube station.

We take the Hammersmith & City line to Upton Park, and I sense something is off with my colleague almost immediately. His posture seems unusual, and it sparks my interest. I observe him as the train glides through the dark tunnels. Egan keeps shifting in his seat as if he can't find a comfortable position.

'Are you quite all right?' I ask, trying to deduce what is wrong with him. Back-pain, maybe.

'Hmm?' He turns his head my way; one eyebrow questioningly raised above his dark glasses.

'You seem kind of... fidgety.'

'It's nothing,' he mutters in a drop-it fashion.

I half-hum, half-grunt in response, my vocal equivalent of a shrug, and redirect my attention to a nearby tourist with a Tube map in his hand. The poor man's holding it upside-down; I motion for him to turn it around.

Egan goes rigid beside me, wilfully so. He manages to keep the charade up for another five minutes before he leans, as discreetly as he can, to his left, and shortly after to his right.

'All right.' I nudge him softly in the ribs. 'What is it?'

'Nothing,' he mutters again, through clenched teeth, as he stills his movements once more.

'Ash?' I say, in my I-won't-give-up tone.

'All right, all right. I fell on my bum when I took the stairs out of my building this morning. Happy?'

I stifle a laugh. 'Are you hurt?'

'It's nothing; it was hardly the first time I've fallen,' he says, flapping a nonchalant hand about. 'I have quite the strong bum, you know.'

This time, I can't help but laugh. 'Clearly.'

He flaps a hand again. 'I'll be fine in an hour or so.'

'You know, if you want me to come by and spend a few days with you, you only need to ask.' I know full well my offer will be rebuked, but make a point of offering anyway.

He snorts in response. 'This isn't the first winter I've had to live through, Alexandra Neve. I've survived worse on my own, thank you very much.'

'Fine, have it your way, but if you manage to break both arms, I'm not spoon-feeding you.'

We take a right at the station's exit and walk past Queen's Market and its mass of chilled consumers and tourists. We continue south on Green Street until West Ham's stadium and take a right turn onto a smaller residential street. We find the home of one Rebecca Doughton near the end of Walton Road.

Mrs Doughton called the agency this morning, with urgency in her voice, and asked for a meeting that very afternoon. She requested that Egan and I come, as soon as we could, for a job of the utmost importance. She refused to divulge more information over the phone, but my curiosity was piqued. I promised her we would honour the appointment — besides, we didn't have any other clients banging down our door.

We stop at the front door of a typical Victorian terrace house, and I press the doorbell. The door swings open before I have a chance to remove my finger from the button, revealing a slim woman in her forties with short, curly hair, high cheekbones and tired eyes. I note in passing she's long overdue for a root touch-up to hide the silver strands eating their way down her brown hair.

She's wearing a wrinkled blouse and a pair of jeans. She beckons us in with a quick, nervous gesture.

'Ms Neve, Mr Egan, please come in.' She leads us to the living room of the small house and has to remove papers from the settee to make room for my colleague and me to sit down.

My stomach clenches as I catch sight of the documents:

missing person posters. I only catch a glimpse of the documents, but the word MISSING printed in bold and capitals is impossible to ignore, and they show a picture of a young girl with dark, wavy hair.

Mrs Doughton drops the leaflets on a nearby table, already filled to the brim, and turns back to face us.

I nod at the notices she just put away. 'Your daughter, I presume.'

'Yes,' the woman says in a tired voice. She sits down, looking both exhausted and distressed. 'She disappeared last weekend. I... I have no idea where she is.'

Egan frowns and asks, 'Have you contacted the police?'

'Of course I have. It was the first thing I did Sunday morning when I couldn't reach her,' she replies, her hands twisting in her lap. 'I called all of Isa's friends, the other dancers, her teachers, everyone in our family... everyone I could think of.'

She takes in a breath and bites at her lower lip. 'No one's seen her, not since Friday afternoon. At first, I assumed she'd spent the night at a friend's, but when I still couldn't reach her on Sunday... She's never been gone so long, and she always calls me back.'

She shakes her head and bites her lip again. 'The detectives think she ran away. I tried to tell them she wouldn't—' she clenches and unclenches her hands nervously, '—I tried and tried to tell them my daughter isn't like that. No matter how it looks, she wouldn't leave me. It's been just the two of us since my husband died three years ago. Isa wouldn't leave. She just... she wouldn't.'

Tears fill Mrs Doughton's eyes, and she seems ready to fall to pieces.

Damn it; I hate jobs like this one. I force an amiable smile, lean forward, and try to get the poor woman's full attention to draw her away from the brink before she falls apart on us. 'Tell us more about your daughter. How old is she?'

In response, Mrs Doughton reaches for one of the missing person posters and places it in my hand while she dabs at her eyes with a tissue.

I find my answer underneath the smiling face of a young brunette with a cheery smile and her mother's dark eyes. I read the words aloud, for Egan's benefit: 'Isabella Doughton, age 24.'

Twenty-four; same as me. I fold the notice in two and place it inside my shoulder bag.

'What's your theory, Mrs Doughton?' Egan asks.

The woman inhales nervously. 'Something must have happened. She wouldn't have left without telling me. She must be somewhere she can't contact me; maybe someone took her or, or...' she falters, not daring to speak her mind any further. It isn't hard to picture what terrible fates a mother in her situation could imagine for her child.

'What makes you so sure she didn't run away?' Egan asks, his brows scrunched.

Although I recognise that my friend tried for a kind, neutral tone, his words came out a little clipped. It's the result of years spent tutoring kids who weren't attentive. Try as he might, he has a hard time keeping the superior know-it-all tone to a minimum.

Our hostess's face darkens at the question, and I fear Mrs Doughton has taken it the wrong way. She opens her mouth, closes it and opens it again, before snapping, 'A mother knows these things.'

She fixes Egan with fierce, unwavering eyes, both furious and aggravated. Her raging emotions are so close to the surface: the grief, the worry, the sleepless nights, the many phone calls and hours of searching, and surely nightmares and too much time spent imagining the worst. She needs support right now, not a tactless PI.

I glance at Egan and see that he's straightened in his seat. From the lines on his face, I know he's misinterpreted her sharp answer, and he looks ready to reply in kind. I place my hand on his forearm, a signal for him to be cautious and ease off a little. He nods, almost imperceptibly, to acknowledge the unspoken command.

'Mrs Doughton,' I keep my tone amiable and open, as I rephrase the query, 'we need to know what caused the police to stop the investigation; what misled them?'

The woman turns her tearful eyes my way, bites at her lower lip, and says, almost reluctantly, 'The clothes.'

I lean forward, wait for her to continue.

She looks down at her hands resting in her lap. 'In her wardrobe, some clothes are missing. Some money is also missing from her savings account.'

Mrs Doughton looks back up with plaintive eyes, and I nod for her to continue.

'It could mean any number of things.' She rushes the words out. 'Isa could have lent those clothes to a friend, or given them to charity. Same thing with the money.' Her voice strengthens as she continues. 'It doesn't have to mean she ran away. Someone took her, Ms Neve. Someone took my little girl from me.'

'Please.' She looks at Egan, then back at me. 'Please, I'll pay.

I'll pay whatever you require, but you have to find her. Find my little girl.'

'Mrs Doughton,' I start, unsure how to phrase my thoughts, 'missing person cases aren't easy to investigate.'

I chance a look at Egan. From his tense expression, I gather he feels the same way. 'We're not used to handling such cases; I'm not sure we're the best suited for this job. Besides, an official police investigation is ongoing; we could get in their way.'

I sigh; this is never easy to explain. I force myself to continue. 'You have to understand; we'd risk doing more harm than good.' Not to mention getting ourselves into some legal trouble, I mentally add.

'You don't believe me, is that it?' the woman asks, straightening her back. She goes from sorrowful to full-blown angry in the space of a second. 'You're like them. You—you think she ran away.' She points a finger at herself. '*I* am her mother. *I* know my little girl. She wouldn't have run away; not in a million years.'

'Mrs Doughton,' I try a placating tone, 'we believe you, but you have to—'

'I thought you would help,' she interrupts. 'You were my only hope.'

The fight leaves her as fast as it came, and she flops back down in her chair, deflated. It doesn't take a professional psychiatrist to see the poor woman is on the verge of a nervous breakdown.

'I thought you could help,' she repeats. 'Thought you would help... you... Isa always spoke so highly of you... I thought you would...'

The mumbled words grab my attention. 'What do you mean, Mrs Doughton?'

Her eyes are once more pleading as she looks back up. 'You know her,' she says, her gaze directed at Egan. 'You know my little girl.'

I bump my hand against my friend's softly to let him know she's addressing him. Egan's eyebrows rise with surprise above his dark glasses.

'I beg your pardon?' he says.

'Isabella Doughton,' the woman repeats the name. 'You know her, Mister Egan; she was your student, three years ago.'

The connection is unexpected, and it visibly surprises my partner.

'I... um...' he starts hesitantly.

'She had two classes with you for a year.' Mrs Doughton cuts in. 'She talked about it a lot. She liked your classes, she did. Isa is a smart girl. She was always a good student, very attentive. Surely you remember her.'

Egan nods. His face is a blank mask, but I spot uneasiness in his posture.

'Only a year?' I ask Mrs Doughton. I find it strange she didn't have classes with Egan throughout her entire course.

'She left university at the end of the first year,' Mrs Doughton explains. 'She loved it there, but she didn't have enough time for it. Isabella is a ballerina; she's been dancing since she was old enough to stand. She's been with a ballet company for many years now. She also teaches young children.

'Please,' the woman turns to face me. 'You don't know her, but my Isa wouldn't have left. She wouldn't have left me; she wouldn't have left her students; she wouldn't have left her dance partners.'

Her words and her sorrow are persuading, but I know we shouldn't take this case, we really shouldn't. 'Mrs Doughton—'

'I remember Isa read in the newspaper that her former history professor became a private detective,' Mrs Doughton's attention once more focuses on my partner. 'That's why I sought *you* out. I thought you, of all people, would care.'

A second or two later, she turns the pleading eyes of a worried-sick mother to me. 'Please, you have to help me. I have no one else to ask. I *know*—' she says the word with fervour '—my little girl didn't run away.'

I'm about to say yes, but Egan beats me to it. 'We'll do our best,' he promises.

2

————

Egan's words and his fervent tone surprise me. He is usually more guarded with his emotions. He is tensed up and, though there's no reason for it, he seems angry. At who or what, I have no clue. Whatever is going on with him, now is not the time. I turn my attention back to Mrs Doughton.

'Has anything out of the ordinary happened recently?' I demand of our new client.

'No, nothing.' She shakes her head.

'Think, Mrs Doughton. Anything can be of importance, even the most insignificant detail.'

She shakes her head again.

'Has she fallen out with any of her friends or fellow dancers? Has she had any problems with her students?'

Mrs Doughton shakes her head again.

Egan sits up then, and I watch him with a raised eyebrow as he takes out his cane. 'I'm deeply sorry, but I have another appointment.' He extends his hand out vaguely in the direction of our client, and Mrs Doughton shakes it. She is surprised too; I can see it.

'Alexandra will continue the interview and fill me in later. We will do our best to find your daughter, I assure you,' he adds before making his way out of the living room.

Mrs Doughton sees him to the door. I watch him go, puzzled. I don't believe his excuse for a second, not with the expression on his face — the cold, emotionless face I'm familiar with. The face which means he's masking his emotions and shielding himself from the outside world. The face I hadn't seen in a while and hate to see. I stand and wait for our client to return.

'Could I see your daughter's room?' I ask as she returns to the living room.

The woman nods and motions for me to follow her up the stairs. On the first floor, she leads me to her daughter's bedroom.

It's simply decorated. The pale shades of beige and pink suggest a girl's room. The low-cut dresses and high heels I find in a cupboard say woman rather than girl. There are several framed pictures on a shelf, of young girls in traditional ballet wear, Isabella and her dance partners. The place is lively yet ordered. I find a few books, Regency Era romance mostly, and a manicure kit on the side of her desk.

The sight makes me uncomfortable; I swallow nervously. Get rid of the manicure kit, replace the boots with Converse trainers, the dance-related items with investigation-related items, and the period romance with some contemporary fantasy and you would have a replica of my bedroom. Only twenty-four years old; *my age*, I think again.

I find no sign of a potential love entanglement, no sign of

distress or impending doom. To me, it seemed Isabella Doughton had little in her life aside from her passion... just like me.

'Dancing is all she is,' I muse aloud.

'She loves to dance,' her mother says, behind me. 'She started as a child, and she showed great promise. My husband and I always supported her decision to take the dancer's path.'

I turn back to face the woman leaning against the door frame. 'Maybe she wanted a change?'

Mrs Doughton crosses her arms over her chest, clearly affronted at the suggestion.

I try to soften my words. 'Look, we said we would investigate and we will, but Mrs Doughton, the life you've described is a strenuous one. Maybe Isabella woke up one day, felt this was all too much pressure and needed a breath of fresh air.' I'm living proof that people can sometimes change their minds quite suddenly. Literature student one day, private investigator the next — my mother still has to get over that one.

'Look, I studied at the same university your daughter did. Like her, I had my future mapped out, but I tossed all of that through the window one day in exchange for an investigator's life. I'm not saying that's what happened with Isabella, but we have to consider that possibility. If she decided to leave, she must have told someone or had some help. There must be a lead we can follow.'

A faint nod was the only concession Mrs Doughton made during my speech.

'Who could she have talked to?' I ask her. 'Aside from you, who did she confide in?'

'All of Isa's friends are dancers.' The woman turns to exit the room. 'Let me get you a pamphlet from her dance company.'

I take another look at the room, observe it carefully and commit details to memory, and then I follow Mrs Doughton back down. I don't have a photographic memory, but I can come close when I want to. I'm a good pencil artist, a skill passed down to me by my father, and I can draw rather well. I've perfected over the years what I call my *snapshot technique*. It consists of taking a mental picture of what's in front of me and drawing it in detail at a later time. That technique works wonders in my new job.

When I come down, Mrs Doughton is waiting by the foot of the stairs with a light-blue pamphlet, held in her trembling fingers. I exchange it for one of our business cards.

'Our fee is four hundred a day plus expenses, and I'll have to ask for a first payment of a thousand pounds.'

She nods, moving to grab her handbag from a nearby table. She writes a cheque with quick pen strokes and hands it to me.

'We'll call with regular updates,' I promise. 'Give us a ring if you remember something, anything.'

I put my winter gear back on. 'We'll start at the dance company, interrogate the other dancers. I'll also make a call to a friend within the Metropolitan Police, see what I can get from them.'

Mrs Doughton thanks me profusely as I leave the comfort of the warm home and return to the biting cold waiting outside.

Still in the porch, I send a quick text to my friend, Detective Stenson, asking him to give me a call. I wonder if there's any chance he can give me more information on Isabella's disappearance. The Metropolitan Police is bound to have a file on her, and I'd love to get my hands on a copy.

Placing the phone back in my pocket, I shove my gloves on, tuck my chin inside my duffle coat and start walking back up the street. To my surprise, I find Egan seated on a bench, twenty yards ahead.

I sit next to him and wait for an explanation that doesn't come. Looking at my own breath fog in front of me, I wait as the cold seeps through my clothes.

'Come on.' I stand up after a good five minutes have passed. 'She gave me the address of Isabella's ballet company. It's a good place to start the investigation. It's on Whitechapel Road.'

Egan remains seated and mute. His face is a cold mask as devoid of emotion as the surrounding air is devoid of warmth.

I stop and reconsider my plan, look at the present situation with a more critical eye. I know Egan hates to share his problems with others — I've never met anyone more private than him — yet, here he is. He chose to wait for me, knowing I would come out, knowing I would want to ask him questions. I take the fact he decided to stay to mean that, for once, he does want to talk.

I take a step closer to the bench, crouch in front of him. 'All right, my friend, talk.'

Egan doesn't move, doesn't reply, but I see him swallow.

'Come on, Ash. You can tell me.'

I hesitate to reach for his hand, unsure how much pushing he will allow.

'I don't remember her,' he says, in a cold monotone that matches the frosty surroundings.

'Isabella?'

He nods. 'Years later, she remembered me when she saw that article in the newspaper, but I don't remember her at all. Not even her name. I didn't mean to lie to her mother, but... how could I tell her I had no idea who she was talking about?'

So what? I'm tempted to ask, but I refrain. I reach for his hand, curl my gloved fingers around his.

'I don't remember much of anyone,' he admits. His words are tainted by a bitterness that has me raising an eyebrow. 'I never cared to remember.'

I sit down next to him, slightly askew so I can look at his face. Egan is my best friend, but he isn't anyone else's. He wasn't Mr Popular at the university; not because of his handicap but because of his attitude towards... well, towards everybody. He didn't care about others, and he was snappy; he mocked and ridiculed a great many students and fellow staff members. It was more than just a coping mechanism to adapt to his condition; I think it was a defence tactic. A way to shield himself from a cruel world that had already hurt him too much — an invisible wall he built to make sure no one would ever dare and try to come anywhere near him and want to form any kind of emotional attachment.

I must have misread the signs because here I am, but even though he has warmed up to me considerably this past couple of months, his list of friends is rather short.

'You can't be expected to remember everyone,' I say softly. 'Hell, I would be hard-pressed to come up with the names of half of my classmates. You had thousands of students over the years. It's okay that you don't remember Isabella.'

Egan shakes his head. 'You don't understand, Lexa. I don't —' he clenches his jaw and pain filters on his face for an instant.

'I don't remember *anyone*,' he finishes. His voice cracks on the last word.

'Save for you, I don't. Not really. You were all—' he waves a hand in front of him '—voices in the crowd. I didn't care to listen to any of you; you were like an annoying background noise. What kind of a professor does that make me? What kind of a man?'

His thin lips draw together in a fine line, pale under the strain. 'I don't know what's in your eyes when you look at me,' he whispers through clenched teeth. 'Hate, pity, indifference?'

The question hurts. Now I understand where the anger I perceived earlier came from. It was aimed at himself. I am reminded of how much he has changed over the past months. This job has not only helped me become someone else; it's helped him too.

'None of those things,' I say. I lean a little closer and run my hand along his shoulder blades. I feel like hugging him, but fight the urge, knowing it wouldn't be welcomed.

'So you were a fool!' I say, the harshness intentional. 'A top-notch arsehole who couldn't care less.'

He winces at the words, tries to pull away, but I don't let him. He needs a metaphorical smack on the head to get him out of his funk, and I intended to deliver.

I grab a handful of the back of his coat to hold him in place. 'Past tense, Ash, damn it. You're not that fool anymore. I wouldn't hang out with you if you were.'

He tries to pull away again, a half-hearted attempt this time.

'That was then — this is now. Now is what matters!' I soften my tone. 'You can continue to wallow in self-pity, or you can try to bring this girl home and make things right.' I let go of him. 'Which will it be?'

He sniffs, whether from the cold or because of my words, I do not know. When Egan and I started to work together, we promised each other ours would be a relationship based on truth and honesty. "No lies, no condescension, no pity, and no free passes." I am a woman of my word.

'Which will it be?' I repeat. 'Are you going to sit on this bench for eternity feeling sorry for yourself — or are you going to get to work?'

He swallows twice, and leans against my side. 'I hate you,' he mutters into my shoulder.

I pat him on the back. 'You're welcome.'

'Whitechapel, eh?' he says, pulling back. 'Would we be better to take the District Line or Hammersmith?'

I chuckle; mission accomplished. 'Whichever train comes first, my friend.'

3

On the walk back to the Tube station, I describe Isabella's room and the pictures I saw. I rehash everything Mrs Doughton told me and convey the impression I got from her of her daughter.

'We have to be careful with this, Lexa,' Egan tells me as we ride the Tube southbound. 'I doubt the Metropolitan Police will take very kindly to us interfering in one of their investigations—' he pauses for effect '—again.'

I blow out a long breath through clenched teeth. 'I'm well aware of that.'

'Still...'

'Still, I suppose that asking around and forming our own opinion on the matter can't be seen as obstructing the course of an ongoing investigation, can it?'

Egan shakes his head.

'What?' I ask. 'It'll just be us talking to random people, who happen to know Isabella. No harm, no foul.'

The train glides to a stop, and we exit, along with a dozen other Londoners dressed in their warmest clothes. A gush of cold, biting wind hits us square in the face, as we escape the stuffy confines of the Underground station.

The ballet company is easy enough to find. The building looks like a renovated old factory. It makes sense; remove the old machinery, get rid of the dust, and you get a big empty space to rehearse in. I'm glad to find it open, even though the Christmas Holidays are fast approaching.

I pause, my hand on the door handle as a thought strikes me. Egan stands behind me, a little to my right, with his left hand loosely holding my right arm. I turn back to face him.

'You've changed, you know.' I pour all the sincerity I can into my words. 'You're not that man anymore — you wouldn't feel regret about not remembering Isabella if you were.' I push the door open, and we enter without exchanging another word on that particular subject.

We walk down a long corridor, and musical notes drift through the air. A piano plays a basic melody I don't recognise, but Egan seems to appreciate it. We follow the sound and find a large rehearsal room. Two of the walls are covered in mirrors; a long wooden horizontal bar has been wrought into the concrete along one side.

There are eight young women in the centre of the room, ranging in age from about twenty to thirty. All of them are wearing leotards, tights and pointe shoes. They stand in line, their hands up on each side of their hips, as if holding up ample skirts. The posture makes them look funny. I suppose a skirt or a dress will be part of their costume when they perform to their audience.

While they hold up their imaginary clothes, the girls' feet do a dance of their own, scissoring at a quick speed — opening, closing, right foot in front of the left and then the other way around, a quick jump and then some more footwork.

The music picks up; they all let go of their invisible skirts, raise their arms wide and high, and break into two groups of four. They move through the room, each group mirroring the moves of the other, before coming back to form one single line in the centre. There's more swirling, footwork and jumps before all the girls stop with one arm arched high above their heads.

I am amazed by their grace and agility, but mostly by their synchronisation. I have no idea how many times they've rehearsed this series of movements, but all the dancers moved as one.

The piano stops, and I cannot help but clap, thus attracting the attention of everyone in the room. I don't care; it's well deserved.

The woman who had been sitting at a black piano, on the far left of the room, stands up with a frown. Her brown eyes narrow at us as she steps closer.

'This is a private rehearsal,' she says dryly, her arms crossed over her chest.

I smile as I take a step inside the room. Feeling self-conscious amongst the group of talented dancers, I force myself to move with as much grace as I can muster — which I fear isn't much. I'm too tall and broad to be gracious. 'My apologies; we didn't mean to interfere in your work, but we're investigating the disappearance of Isabella Doughton.' A murmur of surprised 'oohs' from the dancers punctuates my words.

'We would like to speak with her teacher and dance partners. It won't take long,' I add.

The woman's contempt evaporates at my words, and she asks, her expression serious, 'Are you with the police?'

'Private investigators,' Egan replies. 'We were hired by Isabella's mother.'

At this, the woman relaxes and beckons us in. She appears to be in her mid-forties, her long brown hair showing the first silver strands of age. She has the light-olive skin of a Mediterranean woman.

I step forward, and Egan follows, holding onto my arm. The teacher, who hadn't spotted Egan's blindness, notices now from the way we walk. She doesn't comment on it though.

'I'm Luisa. I run this company.' She reaches a hand out to me.

'I'm Alexandra Neve, and this is my partner, Ashford Egan.' I motion to my friend before reaching for one of our business cards.

'Pleasure to meet you,' he says, nodding.

'Likewise,' the woman says. 'I have spoken a lot with Rebecca, the poor woman. She came here several times to talk with the girls and me. She's so heartbroken.

'Truth is,' she continues, 'I don't understand the situation any more than she does. I see no reason why Isabella would have left. She's a wonderful woman and a passionate dancer.'

'Is she a good dancer?' I ask, nodding at the other women in the room, who are stretching out and chatting with each other now that they have a break.

'Yes, she's a natural,' Luisa explains.

I frown at the word.

'True grace cannot be learned — you either have it, or you don't,' Luisa explains. 'You can learn the steps, you can train to be suppler, but this unique glow... it only shines from some. It cannot be manufactured.'

'Isabella has it?'

'Yes, and she loves to dance. It's in her blood.' She smiles. 'You should see her when she teaches the young girls. She has the patience to show them the same moves over and over again; the kindness and the care she possesses... she has true passion.'

Tears prickle at the corners of Luisa's eyes, and I offer her a sympathetic smile. Something tells me the same passion for dancing runs through the lean woman's veins.

Well, there goes my theory of Isabella wanting to quit the dancer's life. She couldn't have stopped being a dancer, any more than I could stop being an investigator. Time to pursue another angle.

'You were rehearsing *Giselle*, weren't you?' Egan asks.

I have no idea what he's talking about, but Luisa does. Her thin lips stretch into a smile as she nods.

I translate the motion without needing to think about it. 'She just nodded.'

'Ah,' my friend smiles. 'I thought I recognised the melody. Does Isabella play Giselle?'

The woman nods again, catches herself and adds, 'Yes, yes, she does.'

'And who plays the duke?' my partner asks.

'Theo Levain,' Luisa replies, 'and our Hilarion is played by Marc Jules. They're not here at the moment. We were rehearsing a part of the harvesters' dance this afternoon.'

I make a mental note to ask Egan what the ballet is about later on. For the moment, I'm content to let him take the lead.

'The boys will be here when we rehearse the wedding tomorrow.'

'Are you preparing the entire play?' Egan asks.

'Yes, we're going to perform the entire ballet on Christmas day at the Coliseum.' Luisa's expression darkens. 'Now we need to replace our lead; I don't know how we'll manage.'

I frown as a thought strikes me. I glance at the women behind Luisa. I may not know much about dancing, but I've seen *Black Swan,* and it didn't end well for poor Natalie Portman. 'Is there any rivalry among the dancers?' I ask. 'Did Isabella get the part at someone else's expense?'

'No, nothing like that.' Luisa smiles at my question, as if I'd said something silly. 'We're a medium-sized company, and Isabella is by far our best dancer. There was no competition; all the other girls look up to her. I doubt we will be able to find a replacement within the company.'

My lips contort bitterly as another of my bright theories goes down the drain. I only have one left: the love entanglement.

'If you don't mind, we would like to have a word with the other dancers,' I motion to the ladies in the background, 'and those two men you mentioned.'

'Of course,' Luisa nods. 'Anything, if it can help you.'

Egan and I wait for the class to finish, and then spend the better part of an hour talking to the girls. We split up and ask them questions separately. A few of them seem to be gossipy types, but even they have little of interest for us. Knowing Isabella's tastes in music or that she only ever eats cake on her birthday and at Christmas doesn't get us any closer to finding out what happened to her.

We thank Luisa for her time, give her a few of our cards with the instruction to hand them to any of the dancers if they remember anything, and head back outside.

'So,' I push my hands into my gloves again as we walk away from the building, '*Giselle*?'

'A ballet,' Egan indicates smugly.

I snort. 'I guessed as much.'

A few isolated snowflakes fall. I catch one on the tip of my gloved index finger and watch it melt and disappear.

'*Giselle* is a love story, set in the Rhineland of the Middle Ages during the grape harvest.'

'How would you even know that?' I ask as we take a turn into a larger, busier street. My friend moves imperceptibly closer to me. I look at the path ahead of us with care and avoid the urban obstacles with ease.

'I'm a man of many secrets,' Egan replies, a smile in his voice. 'Now, do you want to hear the story or not?'

'Please do proceed, professor.'

'A young farm girl, Giselle, falls in love with a nobleman, Duke Albrecht, who pretends to be a peasant. Giselle is warned off him by Hilarion, a peasant who's desperately in love with her. Despite the warning, Giselle chooses Albrecht and agrees to marry him. There's a huge party, lots of dancing, and happy people, but then—' he pauses dramatically, '—Hilarion brings forth the sword and horn of the duke he found in his cottage, revealing to all his true identity, and Giselle dies of a broken heart.'

'Oh, so it's not a happy story, then,' I mutter.

Egan tsk-tsks me, apparently ticked off that I interrupted him. It reminds me of old times when he was standing at the head of his lecture room. I was seated in the front row listening to him recount old battles with the same interest.

'That was just the first act.' He raises an imperious finger in front of him, a sign I know means I should pay attention. 'The second act is set in a moonlit glade near Giselle's grave. Hilarion is mourning her death, when suddenly he's pursued by female spirits who, jilted before their wedding day, rise from their graves at night to seek revenge upon men by dancing them to death.

'Giselle is summoned from her grave too and, when Albrecht enters, searching for Giselle's grave, she appears before him. He begs for forgiveness. She gives it, and the two dance.'

We stop at a crossing, wait for the lights to change, and Egan's voice darkens as he continues his story. 'Hilarion is killed by the spirits, who then sentence the duke to death. Giselle protects him and thus regains her freedom. Having saved the love of her life, she returns to her grave to rest in peace. The ballet ends with Albrecht realising that Giselle has saved his life, crying at her grave.'

We start walking again. I wait a beat, to make sure I don't interrupt again, before saying, 'Still not a happy story.'

Egan shakes his head with a defeated sigh. He must be disappointed that I don't appreciate the poetic beauty or whatever. My partner is an opera enthusiast, and I'm not surprised he can hold his own in ballet territory. All this cultural, classical stuff is foreign to me. I'm more into rock and music videos. I suppose Egan's strange, outdated tastes could prove useful to this case.

'What did you think of Luisa?' I ask Egan as we go down the stairs of Whitechapel's Station.

'I believed her. She sounded sincere.'

'She looked aggrieved,' I say, confirming that the visual clues match the audio ones. 'It looks like Mrs Doughton is right. I see no reason why her daughter would have wanted to leave.'

Egan nods. 'Maybe the male dancers will be able to shed some new light.'

'Yes. On-stage love may have transposed from the grave into real life — but did our Giselle choose someone? And if so, was it the duke or the peasant?'

4

Theo Levain is a tall man in his early twenties; he is clean-shaven, except for light-brown sideburns. He invites us into his small flat in Shoreditch with a ready smile and a graceful wave of his hand. Everything about him screams dancer — from his long, lean limbs to the grace with which he sits down on the chair he drags from the kitchen. Egan and I share the small living room settee.

'I'm sorry; there isn't much room in here, I'm afraid,' the young dancer apologises, handing us glasses of water.

'It's okay, don't worry,' I say as we place the drinks on our knees, for lack of a coffee table to use.

There's a telly on the opposite side of the room with DVDs piled up neatly next to it. Two piles, I note. I try to decipher the titles and discover that the left pile contains action and science-fiction flicks, while the second contains comedies and romantic tales — his and hers, maybe.

'You wanted to talk to me about Isabella?' Theo asks, and I return my attention to him.

'As my colleague said, we are private investigators. We have been hired by Isabella's mother,' Egan says.

'Anything you can tell us about her, to help us understand the type of person she is, can help us,' I add. 'Of course, if you know anything about her disappearance, that would help too.'

With a grim look, he says, 'I'm afraid I don't know what happened to her. I saw her last Friday morning at rehearsals. She was her usual self. Nothing out of the ordinary happened. I haven't seen or heard from her since.'

'I was as surprised as everyone else when her mother, and later the police, started to investigate her disappearance.'

As Theo speaks, I let my gaze take in the rest of his living room. There are pictures on a shelf to his left. They reveal that our Duke Albrecht has already found his real-life Giselle. Theo Levain is engaged to a curvy, olive-skinned woman who looks nothing like Isabella. Some of the pictures reveal his girlfriend to be an outgoing woman who likes partying and drinking cocktails.

'Do you know if Isabella was seeing someone?' I ask the dancer.

He shakes his head. 'I've never seen Isabella with anyone, and I can't remember her ever mentioning a boyfriend.'

He scrunches his brow in concentration before adding, 'I don't know where she would find the time anyway. She teaches several classes, and the way she dances requires a lot of practice.'

'How much is "a lot"?' Egan asks.

'I exercise at least two hours every day. At times like these, with a show coming up, it's more like four to five. Isabella knew all the steps well before anyone else did. She's the first-to-arrive, last-to-leave type of girl; you know what I mean?'

'What about the other lead dancer? Marc Jules?' I ask. 'Could there have been a thing between them?'

Theo chuckles. 'You haven't met Marc yet, have you?'

'Not yet, no,' I admit.

'He's a nice guy, but Isabella's not his type.' He smiles wryly, before adding, 'Nor would any other woman ever be his type.'

'Oh,' I say, as understanding dawns.

'Do you know if she ever had problems with her students? Any trouble connecting with any of them, maybe someone challenging her authority?' Egan asks.

'I wouldn't know. Everyone seemed to agree that she was a good teacher, though.'

We ask a few more questions that only gather more unhelpful answers, and leave Theo shortly after, without having learned anything useful.

Marc Jules, Giselle's second leading male performer, lives only two streets away, on Shoreditch High Street. Egan and I walk the short distance, sipping at takeaway coffees to warm us up as we go. As we walk past the tall tea building with the word TEA spelled out in giant letters, I feel as if I'm cheating on British tradition with my macchiato in hand.

Marc Jules' flat is pretty much the same size as Theo's, but marginally different at the same time. Where Theo's was full of life, trinkets and mementoes, Marc's barely looks as if someone resides in it. The shelves are bare, no decoration; he hasn't even got curtains.

'Have you moved in recently?' I ask after the introductions are over.

The young man of barely twenty with short blond locks nods nervously. 'Yes. It shows, doesn't it? I haven't had time to decorate.'

He motions for us to sit down at the kitchen table before turning to face the worktop again. I watch him as he pours himself a glass of diet lemonade. His moves are also those of a dancer, elegant and soft, but he lacks the confidence which Theo exudes.

When Marc sits down at the table with us, he hunches forward and clasps his hands together. I note that he brushes his fingers against each other.

'I wish I could offer you tea, but I don't have a kettle yet.' He accompanies his words with an apologetic smile.

'No worries, we had coffees on the way,' I assure him.

'My apologies for the state of the place — I wasn't expecting visitors,' he continues.

'We won't take too much of your time,' Egan says.

'Good location you've got here,' I try, hoping to break the ice.

He shrugs. 'It's okay, I suppose.'

'East End wouldn't be my first choice either,' I force a smile, 'but trust me when I say there are worse places.'

The young man shrugs again. With his shifting eyes, he looks about ready to flee the flat any second. Damn it; in this state, he won't tell us anything.

'And you have your own place too; that's nice.' I try to play the amiable, friendly card, in the hope that it will somehow help him open up to us. 'It's so difficult to find a decent flat these days.'

'Yes, I struggled,' Marc admits. 'Tough times.'

'So,' I say, with a broad smile, 'we've been trying to find more information on Isabella.'

'I didn't know her that well,' he says quickly.

'I know, I know,' I wave my hand nonchalantly, 'but you were training together. She may have let some information slip about plans she had. Friends she was to meet with after classes? That sort of thing?'

'I—I don't know. We never talked, you see. It was just practice, and then we went our separate ways.'

'Of course, I understand,' I say soothingly, as kindly as I can. 'But we need you to make an effort, Marc. Anything she might have said could be useful. Any off-handed comment she could have made in passing?'

'I—I don't know. We didn't hang out together; we never saw each other outside of class,' he repeats, his eyes shifting to the side. 'I want to help you, but I'm afraid I don't know anything.'

'Nothing wrong with that,' Egan says. He bumps his hand against mine. The gesture could be considered accidental, but it was anything but. I rack my brain to try to understand what he wants to attract my attention to. Has it to do with the young man's answer? I replay the words in my head, but find nothing of interest. There's only one explanation, then. Egan's heard something in the young man's voice.

I've learned to trust my partner's ears more than my own. Although I have gotten better since I befriended Egan, I'm still nowhere near as good as he is at picking up lies and deceit in people's voices.

With this information in mind, I take a better look at the

dancer facing us. He looks... fragile more than shy. He has bags under his eyes, his nails show the traces of nervous biting, and his clothes are ill-fitting. Lack of sleep, tension, weight loss. What is going on in Marc Jules' life? What is he trying to hide from us?

'That's not all, is it?' I lean forward, look at him square on. 'There's something you're not telling us. It's plain to see.'

The young man shrinks in on himself even more. 'No... no, nothing. I told you everything I know. I have no idea where Isabella is. I swear.'

A thought strikes me, and I try another angle. 'She obviously means something to you.'

The man's eyes shift to the side as he focuses all of his attention on the half-empty lemonade glass sitting on the table. Gotcha!

'You like her, yet you refuse to help us; it doesn't make sense,' I continue. 'What would Isabella say if she could see you now?'

'I don't know anything,' Marc protests with fervour.

'Really?'

'I'd tell you if I knew. I like her she's my friend. I want to find her too.'

'Then stop lying to us,' Egan says. 'What are you not telling us?'

'If what you're saying is the truth, you would do well to stop keeping things from us. You're slowing us down, Marc; you're wasting our time,' I continue, relentless. I can feel we're close to breaking him, so very close. 'Do you know how valuable time is in a situation like this? Time is everything. Every second we're wasting on you is taking us further away from Isabella.'

'You're letting her down right now.' Egan adds. 'Maybe you're not her friend after all.'

'No — she's my friend. I swear.' Marc rushes the words out, tears welling up in his eyes. 'She helped me when no one else would. I owe her so much.'

My eyebrows rise up at the words, and I cock my head to the side, my expression expectant.

Marc bites down hard on his lip the second he finishes his sentence. He didn't mean to reveal this much to us, but it's too late now. The cat's out of the bag.

I soften my tone now that I've got what I wanted. 'What do you mean, Marc? How did she help you?'

'I don't... she just...' He stops himself and crosses his arms over his chest. 'It's nothing to do with any of this.'

'Let us be the judges of that,' Egan says. 'If Isabella was involved, it could be relevant.'

'It'll stay between us,' I promise. 'We're not the police, Marc. Whatever it is, no one else needs to know.'

The young man lets out a long breath as he uncrosses his arms. Defeated, he lets his hands hang limp in his lap.

'She helped me... Isabella helped me when my boyfriend dumped me,' he confesses. 'It didn't end well... I—I was a mess.'

Marc looks up for a second, and I can see tears in his eyes. I offer him an encouraging smile and nod for him to continue.

'These,' he grabs the hem of his sweatshirt between two fingers, 'are Isabella's. She's the one who helped me move in here. We had plans to shop for furniture together this week.'

'You and Isabella were close friends?' I ask.

He shakes his head. 'No, not really. I transferred from

another dance company earlier this year. I haven't known her that long, and she kept to herself a lot.'

'How did she find out about your troubles, then?' Egan asks.

'I left Rick's flat with nothing but the clothes I had on my back, my wallet, and a large bruise on my chin,' the young man says, shame evident in the bitter tone of his voice. 'I had nowhere to go, so I squatted in one of the rehearsal rooms, slept on a gym mat and used the communal showers. I overslept one day, and Isabella found me when she came in. She made me tell her the truth.'

'And then she helped you?' I ask.

Marc looks up, a thin smile playing on his lips. 'She did. I was very surprised. Like I said, we weren't that close, but she's nice like that. She gave me some clothes — sweatshirts and sweatpants, a few t-shirts that were big enough for me — and a bit of money for food. Later, when she heard one of her students mention a sister going abroad for several months, she enquired about her flat. I moved in here three days later.'

Clothes, money... the pieces of the puzzle slowly came together. 'You didn't tell any of that to the police or Isabella's mother, right?' I ask for confirmation.

Marc looks down at his lap again. 'I couldn't. I... I was too ashamed of myself. My situation, the reasons for it... I didn't want anyone to know. Besides, it has nothing to do with what happened to Isabella. She just helped me get back on my feet is all.'

'Not quite,' Egan says, in a cutting tone.

Marc frowns at him.

'The police assumed Isabella ran away, because some of her clothes were missing and she withdrew a lot of cash recently,' he explains. 'They never considered this could be something else — something more sinister — because of you.'

Marc opens wide round eyes at that. 'What? Wait! No — this has nothing to do with it. It—it— she just helped me out.'

'Well, the police had no way of knowing that, did they?' Egan says, his voice displaying sarcasm a touch too strong for my taste.

Marc's eyes mist over, and he lowers his head in shame. 'I'm so sorry; I had no idea.'

My phone rings, and I fish it out of my pocket.

'It's Matthew.' I stand up, take a step towards Egan, place a palm on his forearm for a second, and move to the entrance door. 'It's probably going to take a while, so I'll take this in the hallway, and wait for you there. It was nice meeting you, Marc.'

My partner nods. The young dancer doesn't give any indication he's heard anything that just happened, and I press the answer button.

'Hi, Matt,' I say, trying to keep the cheeriness to a minimum until I've closed the door behind my back.

'Hey, Alex.' He seems in a better mood than the last time we met.

'How's your case going? Have you guys made any progress?'

'No, nothing. But I did catch a few hours' sleep this morning, so that helps.'

I chuckle. 'Don't overwork yourself.'

'I promise, I won't. If we could only catch a break, though. We found nothing helpful on the crime scene — can you believe it? Not a single trace of DNA, not a hair that wasn't the victim's. This case is so frustrating.' He huffs out a deep breath. 'I got your text. What's up with you?'

My voice finds its seriousness again. 'We just took on a new case... and I need a favour.'

It's his turn to chuckle. 'Favours cost extra.'

'I'll gladly settle my tab whenever you can fit me in, Sergeant.' I blush at my own words, thankful Egan didn't hear that one. He would never let me live it down.

Stenson chuckles again. 'Okay, ask away.'

'Missing persons case. The name is Isabella Doughton, 24, from West Ham. Any chances you can hook us up with whoever is dealing with her case at your end?'

'Hold on,' I hear him move about, and the tapping of fingers on a keyboard. 'Got it. Isabella Doughton, open case... runaway.'

'Her mother hired us; she thinks her daughter was taken, and from the looks of it, seems she could be right.'

'You do know this is an official ongoing investigation right, Alexandra?' Stenson's voice takes a serious tone.

'I know; that's why I reached out to you. I wondered if you could tell me whose case it is.'

I hear him tap a few more keys. 'You got a pencil?'

I hum positively, fish my sketchbook and a pencil out of my bag, and take down the name and phone number he dictates to me.

'I know her; I'll give her a ring,' Stenson promises, 'let her know you check out.'

'Do you think she'll let us have a copy of the file?' I ask, hopeful.

'Official ongoing investigation,' he repeats sternly. 'Of course she won't.'

'Even if I say pretty please?' I question, my voice sickly sweet.

Stenson sighs. 'That might have worked with me, but I doubt it'll work on Lenore Carrington.'

'And there isn't anything *you* can do, right?' I ask, in the same tone.

'No, Alex.'

'Pretty please...'

He sighs again, sounding defeated. 'Fine, I'll see what I can do — no promises though.'

'Thank you ever so much, Sergeant.'

'Don't get your hopes up yet; I don't know if *my* charms will work on her.' He pauses for an instant, and I hear muffled voices in the background. 'Look, I have to go. I'm sorry again for last Friday. I hope I can make it up to you soon.'

'Don't worry, I understand. Call me when you have some free time, yeah?'

'Okay, will do. Don't get yourself into trouble with this new case.'

'I'll try my best,' I say with a sly smile.

While I pocket my phone, I open the building's front door and discover that feeble rays of sun are filtering through the clouds. I pop my head outside and take two steps out onto the pavement. The sun has been all too rare of late; I look up, exposing as much of my face to the warmth as I can to kick up the vitamin D.

When I look back down, a hatchback slowly drives past. I smile as I see the large Christmas tree protruding from the boot. It reminds me I should start decorating our flat. I share a two-bedroom apartment in Camden with my mother and, as per the tradition, we will spend Christmas together. As always with Italians, it's all about the food. It starts with *pasta in brodo*, a stuffed turkey and then a *panettone* accompanied by coffee-flavoured ricotta, filled omelettes, and some *mostaccioli*.

'Why are you humming so happily?' Egan asks, nearing the end of the hallway. I keep the entrance door open, and he steps out on the street on his own.

I close the door, walk to his side and offer him my arm. 'Just thinking about Christmas and food.'

He arches an eyebrow.

'Mum and I always share a home-made three-course meal for Christmas. Boyfriend Bob is going to join us this year,' I tell Egan.

'So it's serious between them?'

'Looks like it.' I'm glad my mother's found someone. Accountant Bob can be a bit soporific at times, but on the whole, he's a nice guy. 'They're talking about moving in together. I suppose it will be on their New Year's resolutions list.'

'Will you keep the flat?' Egan asks.

'No idea. Haven't really thought about it yet, but I doubt I could afford the rent on my own.' I don't mind moving, though. We've only had this flat for a few months — the old one sort of exploded and caught fire because of my job. 'Maybe I should start to look for something smaller in the area.'

We walk in silence for a few minutes before I ask, 'What about you? Any plans for Christmas?'

Egan shakes his head.

'No?' I know he's not very close to his family, but I supposed he would at least go and visit them. 'You're not going to go see your folks?'

'No, I won't,' is all he says. From his tone, I understand I'd better drop the subject.

Why did I even bother to ask? I should have guessed that Mr No Social Life planned to spend the cheeriest time of the year alone in his dreary flat, as if Christmas and New Year's Eve were just any other days of the week. Scrooge!

'You're welcome to come spend Christmas with us,' I offer.

'I'll be fine on my own,' he assures me. Once again, his tone eloquently spells out 'Drop it, Alexandra'.

I decide to redirect our conversation towards more pressing topics. 'Did Marc say anything interesting after I left?'

'No, he just kept apologising. I believe him when he says he has no idea what happened to her.'

'Isabella's mother was right. Her girl didn't run away.'

Egan nods. 'What happened to her then? How does a woman just disappear from the face of the earth without leaving a trace?'

'Someone made her disappear; it's the only possible explanation. We need to go and speak to the police.'

5

Mid-morning the next day, we meet with Detective Inspector Lenore Carrington of the Metropolitan Police, who is handling Isabella's case. She's a short, dark-skinned woman, about forty-five, slender and, at first glance, weak-looking. I do not doubt for a second that her looks must be deceiving. A steely strength courses through her, and she carries herself with the assurance of a woman who knows how to defend herself in any given situation. I wonder if she practises a form of martial art like I do; I bet she does.

She invites us into her office grudgingly, and we sit down on a pair of plastic chairs behind a large glass table opposite her. There's a pile of folders on the left side of her desk and large filing cabinets filled to the brim behind her.

In a straight-to-business, no-nonsense manner, she wastes no time getting to the heart of the matter. 'I don't take kindly to —' she voices the next words almost reluctantly, '—PIs trampling all over one of my investigations.'

Straight-to-business, indeed. I bite my tongue to avoid saying something that may antagonise the situation.

My partner addresses her with his customary cool-headedness, 'Please be assured, DI Carrington, we're merely conducting interviews on behalf of our client, nothing more. Should we come across any pertinent information, we will forward it to you immediately.'

The smartly dressed woman allows a small smile to grace her lips at my friend's words. I take that to mean Egan's answer was satisfactory — it's a good thing I kept my mouth shut then.

'I have crossed paths with DS Stenson a few times. He's a good detective. The only reason we're having this conversation—' she does a back and forth motion with her hand between us '—is because of him. He tells me that, although you two have a terrible lack of, and I quote, "bloody common sense and self-preservation", you seem to have a "copper's instincts".'

I have to smile at her words. I nod, acknowledging the truth of the statement.

A slight incline of her head shows she appreciates my honesty. 'I won't lie to you,' she continues. 'In cases such as these, the first twenty-four hours are critical. They, more often than not, determine how a case will unfold. You find something in that time span... you likely will get some result. Find nothing... and the case grows colder by the hour.'

'You haven't found anything yet, have you?' Egan asks.

'No, we haven't,' she folds her hands on her desk, 'and this is the second reason why I'm inclined to let you investigate this matter further. I suppose two pairs of fresh—' she pauses, seeming to catch herself on the verge of saying something inappropriate, then finishes her sentence regardless '*—eyes* can't hurt.'

Straightforward, honest, and bold — she's not someone to take lightly.

'We'll let you know if either of us spots something you have missed,' Egan replies without missing a beat. His words come without animosity; a sign he too understood her attitude to be the olive branch it was.

Carrington nods, reaches for a file, opens it and peers down at the report it contains. 'We interrogated Isabella's mother, her friends, the other dancers, everyone. No one has seen or heard from her since the 29th. T-shirts and sweatpants were missing from her wardrobe. A little over two thousand pounds was withdrawn from her savings account a week prior.' She closes the file and rests it on the side of her desk again. 'Our theory is that she's a runner. We've issued an alert; her picture is in every railway station and every bus company.'

I nod, thankful for the report, and lean forward. 'We're conducting our own set of interviews. Yesterday, we found out that the clothes and the money weren't for her. One of her fellow dancers, Marc Jules, hit a rough patch lately; she tried to help him out. She lent him some cash and clothes.'

DI Carrington's brow furrows at that. She reaches for the file again, scans through it until she finds the right document. 'That's not what Jules told us.'

'The true curse of the uniform,' Egan chimes in, 'it frightens as much as it inspires respect.'

Carrington's mouth contorts bitterly at the words. She reaches for a pencil and jots a quick note on the document before returning her attention to us.

'Thank you for bringing this matter to my attention.' The words are clipped, but if Carrington is cross with us, she doesn't let it show.

I take it as my cue to ask for more. 'In the spirit of collaboration, is there any chance we could have a copy of your file?'

A deep crease appears between Carrington's brows at that. 'Stenson may be under your spell, but he's the only one. I'm doing him a solid by even talking to you. Now, I will let you continue your investigation because this department lacks manpower, but that's all you're getting. Don't push your luck.'

With that, she stands up in one swift motion. She extends a polite hand for me to shake, and I take it to mean the meeting is over. 'We will speak with Mr Jules again. If he confirms what you just reported, we will angle our investigation accordingly,' she adds, hand still extended.

I stand up too, making an effort to keep my face and tone neutral, and shake her hand. 'Glad we could help. As my colleague said, we're on the same team.'

Carrington reaches lean fingers into her vest pocket and retrieves a white rectangular card emblazoned with the Met's logo. 'My card.' She hands it to me. 'Call me if you find anything else.'

I nod to her, give Egan my arm, and we leave the building without wasting time.

'Well, that went well, didn't it?' he asks as we walk down the stairs.

'Considering she could have had us arrested if she felt like it? Yeah, that went well.'

Egan tsk-tsks me. 'A little rash, no?'

'Sure, it wouldn't have stuck in court, but it would have hindered our investigation.'

Egan waits by my side as I open the front door. I hold it open for him as he walks out, and we find ourselves back on the cold, wintery streets. Snow has started to fall again. I struggle to open my umbrella with my gloved hands. 'Carrington will confirm what Marc Jules told us, and then hopefully her men will interrogate everyone a second time. We need to find another angle to pursue while they do that.'

I open the umbrella over the both of us; to my surprise, Egan takes a rapid step back.

'Wait.' He angles his head to expose his face to the sky and the falling flakes. 'I want to feel it.'

A smile blooms on his face as tiny flakes land on his skin; they're quick to melt away. I chuckle at the sight.

'I remember what snow looks like,' he says with a faraway look. 'I used to like it.'

This statement and the wistfulness that seems to have taken hold of him surprises me.

'Did you ever go skiing?' I ask.

He shakes his head. 'No, but I had a wooden sledge.' He smiles, probably at some distant memory.

I add 'liked sledging' to the short list of things I know about Egan's past.

'There was a small hill close to the house,' he continues. 'Dad and I used to go there in the evenings when there was enough snow.'

As the words leave his mouth, he stops exposing his face to the flakes and takes a step back towards me. The umbrella does its job, protecting the both of us from the snow.

I know Egan well enough to realise that whatever particular memory has just crossed his mind has left a bittersweet after-taste. I also know that the window to the past has closed again, and I won't learn anything more about him today.

'Yeah, kids always love snow,' I state, changing the subject, 'but adults don't like it as much, not when they need to get from A to B in London.' I half-sigh, half-groan. 'I'm sure the Central line's going to be a nightmare if it keeps snowing.'

Egan nods, lifts open the glass of his wristwatch and passes a finger over the clock. 'It's almost noon. Lunch?'

My stomach rumbles at the words, reminding me I skipped breakfast. 'Sure; we can strategise over food.'

My phone chirps at the same moment and I fish it out of my pocket. It's a text from Stenson. 'Drink tonight?' it says.

'When and where?' I type back.

While Egan and I walk to the restaurant, Stenson and I text back and forth and arrange to meet at our usual pub, *Luigi's*, which is not far from my flat, at seven. I pocket the phone with a large smile.

———

'So,' I tell Egan after wolfing down a large bite of pasta, 'I think it's time to assume this case is a kidnapping. Isabella would never have walked away of her own free will. We've established this much.'

'The police will soon come to the same conclusion,' he says.

'Undoubtedly. Now, there have been no demands, and her body hasn't shown up in some back alley.'

'The kidnapper still has her – but why?'

'We can eliminate money, so what is there left? It was personal; she was targeted... maybe some psycho admirer?'

'Someone she knows, then?'

'Someone who left no trace. It must have been planned... Someone who studied her habits... someone who followed her.'

Egan frowns over his plate. 'A family member, a friend, maybe?'

'The police talked to them already. So did we. If she had a stalker, someone must have noticed him. We need to talk to everyone again and see if they remember odd encounters.'

Egan and I spend the afternoon on the phone. We call the relatives, the friends, the students, and frustratingly go no further than the police have. I give up at around six in the evening, bid Egan goodnight and head back up to Camden Town.

Luigi's is a small bar on Camden High Street. It has a long bar with assorted bottles stacked behind it, a few wooden tables and one cheeky, bubbly Italian man who acts as owner and barista.

As I enter the bar, I find Stenson engaged in an animated discussion about football with the owner, Luigi. I sit down at the counter, next to the detective.

'Hey there, stranger,' I say to Stenson, before turning to the Italian. '*Ciao*, Luigi. How's business?'

'Same old, same old,' the barista replies with an easy smile. 'People come, people go. Only two more weeks and it's the holidays.' He laughs heartily. 'Two weeks off — nothing to do but have too much food, too much drink and watch trashy films on telly.'

I smile back. Egan and I are regular customers, and Luigi

became a friend after we helped him get rid of an employee who had a nasty habit of helping himself to money from the till. His bar became a makeshift office for us.

'Hey, have you heard that phone shop's going to close?' Luigi grabs a towel and starts to dry glasses. 'I'm telling you, that place changes its name so often, I can never remember what it is.'

'Which one? Is it the one below my flat or the one down the street?'

He tosses the towel over his shoulder in one swift motion. 'The one in your building. Didn't you see the signs? I walked past it this morning myself.'

'No.' I shake my head. 'Haven't noticed.'

'Some detective you are, *ragazzina*,' he chuckles.

Stenson laughs along, and I punch him lightly in the arm. 'It was dark when I left the flat this morning, all right?'

I'm not looking forward to having new neighbours. For one, it means another moving truck is soon going to be parked in front of my door, blocking the way. Second, a lot of furniture is going to be pushed, dragged, dropped, tinkered and thrown at the oddest of hours. I feel my shoulders sag at the prospect.

'I just hope they don't decide to open some kind of shop that sells food there. I'd hate to wake up to the smell of some greasy oil or spicy curry.'

'Doubt the place is big enough for that,' Luigi says with a frown. 'Last time I went in, it was a locksmith's. It's very small, and there's nothing aside from electricity.'

He reaches for a clean glass and gives it a polish. 'It takes all kinds of equipment to sell food, you see. Lavatories, running water... there are regulations.' He winks at me. 'Trust me, I know.'

Glass in hand, he reaches for a bottle of gin and pours a measure. He tops it with tonic before handing it to me — G&T, my favourite.

I take it and raise it in salute. 'Hope you're right, my friend.'

'You bet,' he says, nodding. 'It could fit a PI agency's office, though.'

With that said, he leaves us to attend some customers who've just entered. I watch him go, feeling dumbfounded.

'So,' Stenson starts, a little awkwardly, 'how are you doing?'

'Fine.' I take a sip of my drink. 'And you?'

He nods and purses his lips before saying, 'Look, Alex, I'm sorry I had to cancel last time. I—'

I stop him with a raised palm. 'Don't worry, Matt. I told you, it's okay, honestly. With our jobs, we know it happens sometimes.'

A large smile complete with dimples rewards my under-standing — it even reaches his almond-shaped eyes. Stenson has one of those smiles to die for. Pearly-white teeth, thin lips, deep dimples, all of which are framed by perpetual three-day stubble that covers his chin and the hollow of his cheeks.

I smile dumbly at him in response.

He takes a leisurely sip of his beer, apparently oblivious to the effect he has on me.

I mentally kick myself and force my hormones to relinquish the hold they have on my brain. 'So, how's your case progressing?'

His smile disappears, seriousness darkening his blue eyes. 'It's taken an unexpected turn.'

I frown at his serious tone.

'We found another victim,' he continues.

I'm surprised. I haven't read anything in the papers yet. 'So soon! The first victim was killed — what? Only a few days ago.'

'No, no.' He shakes his head. 'It's the other way around. We found a previous victim we linked to Carlie Egger; same modus operandi, but killed six months ago.'

I take a long sip of my drink and ponder my friend's words. 'I don't mean to criticise your work, but shouldn't you have made the connection days ago if it was the same MO?'

Stenson's face darkens. 'Yes, we should. We have extensive databases; that crime should have been flagged by our system right away.'

'And yet...' I prompt him.

'And yet, we only found the connection today, and by accident.'

I raise an eyebrow at that. 'How so?'

'One of the guys in our lab... his brother worked on the first crime, and he'd heard details that were never made public. He came to see Langford this morning, suggested we look into it.'

Detective Inspector Langford is Stenson's superior. He is a perpetually ill-tempered man who hates the sight of me. 'That must have gone well.'

Stenson exhales loudly. 'He went berserk. He gave us all an earful for our incompetence; threatened to get us fired and suspended.'

Having met the man, and being on the receiving end of more than one of his rants, I can't help but smile and sympathise. 'Usual day at the office, then.'

The corner of Stenson's lips curl into a short-lived smile.

'Langford was right, though; I don't understand why Sanderson's file, the new victim, didn't show up earlier. Thing is,' Stenson runs a weary hand through his dark curls, 'it wasn't even on the computer. I had to go to some colleagues for the physical file and make copies.'

I have no idea how their system works, but I picture some huge database that works with keywords. Couldn't there have been a malfunction somewhere? Everyone makes mistakes now and then. 'Maybe someone forgot to log it in your Metropolitan Google? It happens.'

Stenson takes a deep gulp of his beer and grumbles, 'It shouldn't.'

'Anyway, you have that case now, the... Sanderson case?' I force myself to sound cheerful. 'Surely that must be of help, right?'

Another quick, joyless smile, 'Dawn Sanderson, age 19, choir singer, reported missing on the 20th June,' he recounts in a monotone voice, as if reading off a file. 'Found dead in the Church of the Living God, on Mile End Road, a week later. No witnesses. Hundreds of DNA samples collected, countless complete and partial fingerprints found on the scene. Actual status of the case six months later: open.'

He downs the rest of his beer in one go, a grim expression on his face. 'No, that doesn't help us. It just proves the murderer has killed before, and that he or she may kill again.'

Stenson waves his empty glass at Luigi before setting it back on the counter.

'From what I heard, the hierarchy isn't very happy with this new development. They're keeping things quiet for now; afraid the press might hear about it. Nothing scares them more than the prospect of reading "Serial killer loose in London" as *The Sun's* next headline. Not to mention what would happen if the press found out we lost a case in a cold case pile.'

I nod in sympathy. 'You're all in a tight place right now. I get it.'

He shakes his head. 'I hate high-profile cases. The minute the press gets a whiff of it, everything becomes more complicated.'

Luigi places a fresh beer next to the sergeant and, with another bubbly laugh, leaves us be again.

'Come on. You must have something to go on?' I prompt Stenson, hating to see him so down.

'That's the thing — we don't. For all the theatrics and the staging, we found nothing that could help us identify the perpetrator. For God's sake, the guy wheeled a grand piano into that damn building without leaving a single print behind.'

'What about the first victim, Dawn...'

'Dawn Sanderson. She was found in the church she sang at, dressed in her choir's uniform. She was propped up with her mouth open — arms spread wide as if she was in the middle of *Oh, Happy Days*. Her eyes...' Stenson swallows, unable to finish his sentence. He reaches for his drink, looks down at it and seems to change his mind. He pushes the glass to the side, a sickly look on his face.

I'm almost afraid to ask. 'What's with her eyes?'

The young man looks back up, meets my gaze with an expression of part disgust, part sadness. 'They were stitched open, Alex. Same as Carlie's. That's how we know it's the same killer.'

That was not reported in the press. My stomach somersaults as the visuals assault me.

'Don't even try to imagine what that looks like. It's just... so wrong.' Stenson pauses, swallows again, his expression even more sickly. 'Just plain wrong.'

I look down. 'Too late.'

'Who does that?' he asks, anger rising. 'Who stitches people's eyes open once they're dead? Sick bastard!'

I have no answer, so I remain silent.

'Poor girl. She had the voice of an angel and her whole life ahead of her,' he mutters, reaching for his beer. This time he takes two long gulps before setting the drink back down.

He reaches for my hand. 'I'm sorry, Alexandra. I'm not very good company tonight, am I? We're supposed to be having a good time, and here I am, talking about the most gruesome case of my career.'

'It's okay.' I look up at him, meet his tired blue eyes. 'I wish I knew how to be more supportive.'

He sighs again. 'I just wish we had more to go on, you know? All we have is a weak victim profile. Both were talented women and from East London.

'Dawn first, a singer and star of her choir. Then Carlie, an accomplished pianist on her way to becoming a famous soloist.' He pauses. 'Makes you wonder what talent he'll pick next.'

Stenson's hand feels warm wrapped around my own. It makes me realise my blood has gone cold as the detective's words keep echoing in my ears.

'Was she kidnapped first?' I blurt out.

The question visibly surprises Stenson. 'Who?'

'Dawn. Was she kidnapped?' I ask, feeling the blood run out

of my face as I dredge the conclusions from my mind.

'Yes, she'd been missing for a week. Why?' Stenson sounds concerned; he grabs my hand with a little more strength. 'What's going on, Alex? You're pale — are you all right?'

I nod, unable to speak for a moment. I see the links in my head, bright lights connecting the dots; it's like a thunderstorm in my brain.

'First Dawn, the chorister, then Carlie, the pianist. And now—' I try to swallow, but my throat has become impossibly dry '—Isabella, the ballet dancer.'

I look up into Stenson's eyes. 'Your killer has already taken his next victim: Isabella Doughton. If we don't find her in time, she's going to be the star of a third macabre instalment.'

'Isabella Doughton? The case you and Egan are investigating?' Stenson asks, aghast. 'What makes you think it's connected?'

'Think about it, Matthew. I've talked with her friends, her teachers. They all agree she's an amazing dancer; she has something special. She's a natural — the star of the show. She is in the same age range as the other two victims, and one day—' I snap my fingers '—she just vanished from the face of the earth. It all fits.'

Stenson frowns, but his curiosity is clearly piqued. He's sitting straighter, fully attentive now. 'I thought she ran away.'

'She didn't. DI Carrington ruled that out when we brought her new information. Trust me, Matt; Isabella is the next victim.'

Stenson fishes his wallet out of his pocket, leaves two tenners on the bar and stands. 'We need to go to the Yard, right now. Langford has to hear this.'

6

'What was so urgent it couldn't wait?' Egan asks as he lets me into his flat at the crack of dawn the next day.

'Major breakthrough in our case.' I stomp forward, sit on the edge of his settee and start to clear the living room table.

'Lexa?' Egan asks hesitantly.

'Can you make some coffee — a large pot, and strong too?'

He retreats to the kitchen with a muttered, 'Some days...'

I reach into my shoulder bag and grab the files I brought along, spreading them out on the table. I had to go through a battle of wills with Langford to get hold of these. However, though he still dislikes me, the grumpy DI had to admit that I had brought them their first real lead in their case, so it was worth a little reward — that and the fact I must have caught him on one of his rare good days.

My friend returns minutes later with a pot of coffee and two mugs.

'Thanks.' I dive for a mug and the pot the second he sets it down on the coffee table.

I don't know how, but Egan manages to grasp my arm as I do. His fingers clasp around my wrist.

'Alexandra, what is going on?' he asks in a no-nonsense voice. 'Why are you so hyped-up? As a matter of fact, how many coffees have you already had this morning?'

I have to smile at the question, despite his serious tone. 'Don't know, lost count. I've been up all night.'

He lets go of my arm now that he has my attention. 'What's going on?'

I force myself to sit back and take a deep breath in an attempt to calm down. 'I met with Matthew last night. He told me about his case, and I realised the two are linked.'

'You mean the dead pianist?'

'And the dead chorister.'

'What dead chorister?' he asks, surprised.

I reach for Dawn's file, and summarise my theory.

Egan's hand comes up to scratch at his chin. 'A singer, a pianist and a dancer...'

I hum. 'All three exceptionally talented. All three gone missing without a trace. All three close to twenty years old and from East London.'

'It does seem to add up.' He pauses, and I picture the cogs in his brain turning. 'How long before the bodies were found?'

I reach for the oldest file, flip it open. 'Dawn went missing on the 20th of June; she was murdered eight days later. Carlie disappeared on the 15th of November; her body showed up in the factory on the 28th of the same month, a few hours after her death.'

'Mrs Doughton said she last saw her daughter on Friday. That was the 29th, wasn't it?'

'The day after Carlie died, yes,' I confirm.

'So the killer kept Dawn captive for eight days and Carlie, for thirteen days.'

I do the math in my head. 'Isabella has already been missing for eight days; we don't have much time left.'

'Have you got both files?' Egan asks, his finger pointing vaguely at the coffee table.

'Yes, Matthew gave me copies before I left New Scotland Yard this morning.'

'And Langford was okay with that?' he asks with evident surprise.

'Not at first,' I smile despite myself. 'Of course, if anyone asks, you never saw these.'

A wry smile appears at the corner of Egan's lips. 'Shouldn't be too hard for me.'

I allow a chuckle before growing serious again. 'We've been looking at these all night; there's not much to go on.'

'They still have zero suspects in either case. No prints, no DNA found on the scene. On the positive side, this will be the first time they get a chance to investigate before the victim is killed.'

'They're taking the case over from Carrington?' Egan asks, surprised.

'From what I understood, yeah, I think so. They'll go over the interrogation rapport, look at everything again from a new angle.'

'Read it all to me,' Egan demands. 'Describe the rest as best as you can.'

I take a long gulp of coffee and begin with the first post-mortem. The chorister was found dead near the church's altar. Nylon cords were used to keep her propped up. She had been dressed in choir clothes, not her own, but some that were identical to the ones every choir member wore. Cause of death was a broken neck, and her eyes had been sewn open, post-mortem. No other injuries, no evidence of sexual abuse.

Carlie was found dead seated at her piano, with a broken neck and broken fingers. Her eyes were also sewn open; no other sign of injuries. She, too, was wearing clothes she'd wear for a live performance — a black robe, a similar style to those found in Carlie's wardrobe, though her boyfriend confirmed it wasn't one of hers.

Egan remains focused and silent throughout, except for a few requests for clarification when I describe the evidence pictures to him. I continue with numerous interview reports, and time flies.

Sunlight bathes the living room in bright light as I close the last file. A glance at my watch reveals that it's already past noon.

'That report was the last one,' I mutter, dropping the file onto the table, which is now a mess of half-opened files, notes jotted down on paper and gruesome post-mortem photographs.

Egan sits still and quiet on his chair. His skin looks paler than usual underneath his long ginger curls. I reach for his arm. 'Are you all right?'

'Yes, sorry. It's just—' he doesn't finish his sentence. He doesn't need to. I feel as uneasy as he does. It's a good thing both my breakfast and lunch consisted of black coffee.

'You're lucky not to be able to see this, Ash,' I admit. 'It's ugly.'

I know these images will haunt me for a long time. Dawn Sanderson had been wearing a pearly-white dress; it ended up stained red, as blood ran down her cheeks from the wounds on her eyes, and along the lengths of her arms because the nylon cords broke her skin. Carlie Egger's thin deft fingers had been crudely broken so it would look like she was playing. She also had tears of red running down her cheeks.

Egan nods half-heartedly. 'Their eyes...' he falters, looking queasy.

I pat his hand reassuringly, not surprised this particular detail touched him the most.

'They—' he swallows, nervously '—you said they were sewn open?'

'Yes.' I take in a deep breath and muster the courage to describe the pictures DI Langford pushed in front of me with a certain delight last night. Stenson didn't want me to see them, but his superior insisted, saying that if I wanted to stick my nose into this case, I had to know everything about it. My stomach had lurched violently at the sight of glazed-over eyes and butchered upper lids.

'Both victims had their eyes stitched open with black nylon, done with a thick needle. Thankfully, it was done after their deaths. A very crude job, reportedly — whoever did this had no medical background. There were four sutures on each upper eyelid.'

'What were they made to look at?' Egan asks with a small voice.

I look up to him at that, surprised. 'Why do you ask?'

'Why else force their eyes open, if not for the victims to look at something?'

Damn! I hadn't thought of that last night. None of us had. I reach for the crime scene pictures from both murder scenes. 'Carlie was looking right ahead, and a little to the side. Dawn was looking ahead too; from the way her head was angled, she'd have looked straight at where the audience sits... just like Carlie, actually.'

'He made them look at him,' Egan says, disgust evident in his tone. 'He forced them to keep looking at him, even in death.'

I try to picture it: a man sitting in the darkness, in front of those puppets made of flesh and bones, watching them for hours — the dead actors of the most macabre of plays — and they had to return his stare. 'I suppose he did, yes.'

Tears surge in my eyes. 'Who could be so twisted? Damn it!' I sit up hastily. My stomach lurches, and I'm thankful again not to have eaten recently. I need some air and walk to the nearest window to open it. Standing there with my eyes closed, I force myself to erase the images from my mind. A light breeze cools my face, but it does little to alleviate the feeling of sickness.

Egan follows me a little while later, and his hand settles awkwardly on my shoulder. He remains quiet as he stands behind me. There isn't much to say, I guess, but his presence is comforting.

'Does it ever strike you as strange?' I ask, once I manage to swallow the bile. 'What our lives have become, I mean?'

He takes his time before replying. 'I've always known humans to be capable of everything — the very best and the very worst alike. History taught me that.'

'Do you ever miss it, teaching?' I ask.

He takes time to consider the question before replying.

'Sometimes I do. It was simpler, easier. But now I see that all it used to make me feel was hollow.'

I lean back against him, and he lets me, before dropping a light kiss on the top of my head. 'Keep looking at the bigger picture, Lexa. Remember why we are doing this.'

I think of Mrs Doughton, alone in her home with her missing person notices and grief-stricken face. The police are updating her, and I'm glad not to have to do it; I hate to be the bearer of bad news.

I think of Isabella, alone in the dark somewhere, the prey of a twisted mind. I straighten my back, determination settling in. 'We have to bring this girl back home for Christmas, Ash. We have to.'

7

I wake up with a start; pain spreads through my left arm, and I moan at my discomfort.

'Are you awake yet?' someone asks me. I need a few seconds to recognise Egan's baritone and blink my eyes open.

'Amawake,' I mumble, and massage my sore arm. 'Did you just hit me?'

'Nope,' he grins, setting his now folded cane back on the low wall behind the settee.

'Right.' I sit up. 'What's so important you've taken to physically attacking your partner?'

'I have something.' He walks back to his chair and motions to the coffee table with one hand. Amidst Stenson's files, left spread all over the table, I find new documents.

'City map?' I grasp the first one and look at the printout — it's of the borough of Islington.

'Did you know,' Egan asks, 'that, by the 19th century, many

music halls and theatres were established around Islington Green?'

'I had no idea.' I place the map cut-out on the table and pick up the second sheet of paper. It is a reprint of a newspaper article; its headline reads "Lloyd's Music Hall Closes: Last Curtain Call Tonight".

'That very establishment,' Egan points his finger in the direction of the document I'm holding — well, he aims at my left knee, but I get the meaning of the gesture — 'was used for concerts, balls and public meetings. But, alas, all good things come to an end. Lloyd's Music Hall became a factory in the eighties, before the new owners went bankrupt and the building was left abandoned.'

I look at the article again, find a street name and then look at the map, realisation dawning. 'That's where Carlie's body was found, isn't it?'

Egan nods, a little smugly.

'So that abandoned factory was a music hall back in the day?' I ponder the thought. 'Do you think the killer knew? Did he bring her there because of that?'

'A chorister found in a church, a pianist found in a music hall...'

'I can see a pattern.' Egan may not be the best when it comes to pop music and hit movies of the moment, but his knowledge of the old, obscure and/or little-known keeps amazing me. 'How the hell did you find that?'

'I know a thing or two about this city's history, young girl.' The corners of his lips turn up into a grin. 'It was just a hunch, but I'm glad it paid off.'

I look down at the article in my hand. It's a scan of the

actual 1981 article. The scan is of low quality with some of the lettering faded or distorted. Some words are hard to make out, even to my good eyes. There is no way Egan's scanner could have allowed him to translate any of it to an audio file. 'No, seriously,' I ask. 'How did you find it?'

'Fine, I cheated,' he shrugs. 'I called a friend, Charles, who's an old London expert. I told him what I was looking for, and a while later he emailed me the map and the article, but—' he holds out an imperious finger '—it was my idea.'

'Duly noted, sir.' I chuckle. 'I'll call Matthew to let him know.' A thought strikes me, 'if it's not too early.'

Egan tsk-tsks as he walks past the couch towards the kitchen.

'What time *is* it, anyway?' I look down at my watch and find it to be close to eleven in the morning. 'Gosh, I don't even remember falling asleep.'

'Are you hungry?' my partner's voice drifts to me from the kitchen.

My stomach grumbles in reply as I stand. 'Starving. I can't remember when I last ate. I think I had an apple before going out to meet Matthew.'

A warm omelette and slices of bacon welcome me when I enter the kitchen after a quick shower.

I sit down at the table with an appreciative, 'Thanks.'

'You're quite welcome.' Egan sits opposite me.

'I had a thought,' I start, after taking a bite. 'Dawn Sanderson was the first victim, and then nothing happened for four months. Then he killed Carlie and kidnapped Isabella the next day. It doesn't fit.'

'Do you think there are more victims? Could the police have failed to make the connection again?'

'No, I doubt it.' I take another bite and wash it down with some coffee. 'I wonder if Dawn was a crime of opportunity. What if it wasn't planned — she was the first one after all... What if, afterwards, our killer took his time to plan his next move? That would explain why there was such a long gap between victims one and two, but there wasn't any between victims two and three. What if he's now working off a list?'

'The three girls had never met yet they shared common traits,' Egan muses. 'He took the time to search for his next victims and find the locations to set up his stages.'

'Dawn was left in the church where she sang every weekend. There wasn't much planning in that,' I say, taking another sip of coffee. 'Unlike that factory, which you've discovered used to be a music hall. I doubt many people knew about that unless they put in some extensive research.'

Egan places his cutlery down before pushing away from the table. His closed eyes and taut face betray a deep level of concentration. I wait for him to share his thoughts.

'When I lost my sight,' he begins, and the change of topic surprises me, 'it was very difficult for me. Of course, it didn't happen overnight; I saw a little less each day. But one morning... I woke up, and the world was gone.'

My breakfast sits forgotten on the table as I turn all my attention to Egan. In all the time I've known him, he's only mentioned the moment he lost his sight once, and very briefly.

Egan stands and takes a few steps away from the table. He's clearly uncomfortable and a little reluctant to broach the subject. He takes a deep breath and soldiers on. 'I had known for years that it was going to happen. I had been warned, and had seen specialists to prepare for it, but still... it frightened me. I was alone in this fight. My father saw me as a lost cause, and my mother kept trying to find a cure that didn't exist.

'The day I lost my sight, I refused to leave my room ever again; I didn't want to go outside anymore. The world was still the same, but to me, it suddenly seemed like a very scary place.' Egan's lips contort bitterly at the admission. 'My mother cried, begged, and cried some more. She wanted me to go see more specialists. She was certain one of them would have the miracle cure and would know how to fix me. She even had some come to the house. My father buried himself in his work, losing all interest in me...' Egan shrugs his shoulders.

I would have a thing or two to say about his parents' poor reactions, and it explains why he isn't keen to go home for Christmas. I keep my mouth shut, though; this is the first time my friend's spoken of his childhood, and I don't want him to stop.

'I got over it, eventually. I learned how to move about my room, then I got comfortable within our house, and I slowly extended my universe. Going one step further every day,' Egan finishes.

I take a few seconds to mull over his story, and look for the deeper meaning of his words. 'Do you think that's what our killer is doing? Moving farther away from his comfort zone?'

Egan walks back to the kitchen table and stops near his chair to rest both hands atop its back. 'Isn't it what we all do?'

I concede the point. 'Your theory places the church at the centre of his comfort zone.'

Egan nods. 'Ground zero.'

'Fancy a walk down Mile End Road?' I ask, already knowing his answer. He nods, and I stand with a smile. If Egan's theory is correct, this would be our first step forward in this case in days.

When we exit Egan's flat a little while later, I find the streets are, once more, covered in white snow. I reach for my friend's arm and halt him at the top of the stairs. 'It's snowed again. Close to two inches — *porca vacca*, will it ever stop?'

Egan inches closer to me and grabs my arm before we descend the stairs.

The air is bitingly cold, and white clouds hang low in the sky. I fear that more snow may fall before the day is over. All that talk about global warming has me smiling mildly. I don't know where it's warming up, but it's definitely not London.

My phone beeps. I look down to find a text from Stenson. 'Matthew says they will establish a list of every place related to dancing and ballet in East London. He'll get us a copy.' We turn right towards the Underground station. 'If they can find where the killer plans to stage his next murder, they have a chance of catching him before Isabella dies.'

'They will have a lot of ground to cover,' Egan sighs. 'It might not be something as obvious as a former theatre. More importantly, we don't know when he plans to...'

'Kill Isabella,' I finish for him. 'You're right. According to the reports, both victims were kept nourished and hydrated; they showed minimal signs of abuse — apart from the broken neck and that thing with their eyes.'

A cold burst of wind hits us after we round a street corner, and I try to tighten my coat around me. Damn, but is it cold today.

'Why keep them healthy for so long?' Egan asks.

'I don't know. Maybe he keeps them in good shape so they can perform for him? It would make sense.'

'Then why kill them, if he wants them to perform?'

I look at the white ground in puzzlement, but no answer springs forth. 'No idea; maybe he grows bored after a while, or the girls stop playing his sick game... Either way—' I swallow '—Isabella's time is running out.'

8

The Church of the Living God is a rectangular building facing north in its small grounds on Mile End Road. It appears to be rather dilapidated but is still standing.

We climb three concrete steps leading to the recessed rectangular opening with a double door that I push open. The air inside is barely warmer than the cold winter air outside.

I look around and find every pew empty. Sunday morning mass must be over already.

'No one around,' I half-whisper to Egan. Churches, much like hospitals, always make me feel uncomfortable. As we walk forward, I yearn to go back outside.

'Is there a door that would take us backstage? Or stairs maybe?' Egan asks in a similarly low tone.

I frown at his use of the word "backstage", but don't comment. Jokes and laughter don't belong here. I look past the pews, behind the stone columns rising from the floor, and spot a wooden door to the left of the first row of pews.

'This way.' I step forward, and Egan follows me closely. Our steps echo on the hard stone floor.

I knock at the wooden door and push it open when no one answers, peering through. 'Staircase.'

An old staircase spirals up and down from the landing we're standing at. The stone steps are old and worn. A cold draft of wind blows down the shaft.

'Hello?' I call out. 'Anybody home?'

'Someone's coming,' Egan says, a few seconds later.

He stops me short from shouting again. I listen, but don't hear anything.

A beat later the footsteps of light feet coming down the stairs echo around us and a middle-aged nun greets us with an engaging smile a minute later.

'How can I help you?' she asks, apparently not at all angry that we have disturbed her.

I introduce us and slip one of our cards into her hand. She introduces herself as Sister Anne.

'You're here about Dawn, aren't you?' the nun asks, placing the card in the pocket of her dark robe without looking at it. 'That poor, sweet child. Such a horrible event... here of all places.'

I see her eyes tear up, and I nod. 'We're sorry to bother you, Sister Anne, but we believe whoever killed Dawn killed another woman a few days ago.' The sister pales at the words. 'He has kidnapped a third young girl, and holds her captive as we speak.'

She crosses herself nervously, 'Oh, dear Lord, have mercy on us all.'

'Sister Anne, we wanted to talk to you about Dawn. We

believe the killer may have been one of your parishioners. He may have met her here, in this very church.'

The nun gasps and falters. 'This is a sanctified home, a refuge to those who seek the presence of our Lord. Many come and go; I couldn't say that I know them all.' She takes in a shuddering breath. 'I cannot believe, for one instant, that one of God's children could commit such atrocious crimes. However lost a soul may be...'

'Sister Anne,' Egan interrupts, 'can you think of anyone who ever seemed suspicious? Someone who behaved strangely? Or someone who showed a special interest in the choir members, Dawn in particular?'

The distraught woman shakes her head. 'I can't think of anyone in particular. Dawn was our best singer, yes.' She smiles reminiscently. 'She had the voice of an angel. Many congratulated her, admired her even. But, I can't think of anyone ever showing ill intent towards her. I'm sorry; I fear I am not much help.

'I locked the church that night, at ten in the evening, as I do most nights. When Father Paul opened up the next morning...' she lets her sentence go unfinished, a veil of sadness falling over her face.

'We're sorry to force you to relive that event, Sister Anne,' I apologise, not knowing what else to say. I feel like cursing this new dead-end, but that can wait until we get outside.

Having nothing more to offer to us, Sister Anne accompanies us back to the front door. We thank her for her time and bid her a good day.

Outside, we are reacquainted with the cold wind and slippery streets. The snow is hard under our boots, turned into ice by the cold. Egan remains very close to me as we walk back to the Underground station, cautious of the way he places his feet on the treacherous pavement.

Before we round the street corner, I look back at the church and catch sight of the nun. She's still on the top entrance step, despite the cold. She has her rosary in her hands, and her lips are moving quickly. I wonder if she may be saying a prayer for us; I suppose that couldn't hurt.

'What's on your mind?' I ask Egan when we near the next corner and he hasn't said a word.

'Hmm?'

'You're quiet. Everything okay?'

'There's something...' he starts, then stops talking.

I turn to face him, curious. 'Yes?'

He frowns under the hood of his coat. 'I can't quite put my finger on it.'

'About the case?' I slow down our pace as we near a small heap of snow haphazardly thrown on the pavement. Some house owner has apparently ploughed the snow off his drive and carelessly piled it on the pavement.

Testa di cazzo, I inwardly curse in Italian; some people can be selfish pigs. There's traffic on the road, so I have to help Egan climb over the piles.

'About Sister Anne,' Egan replies, as we resume walking at a safe pace. 'Did you notice anything odd about her?'

I take an instant to think back on our meeting with the Catholic nun. 'No. She's your average nun, I suppose. Close to fifty, I'd say, with a kind, amiable, round face. The maternal type; she reacted very emotionally to what we said. Her distress showed on her face, in her body language.'

Egan hums contemplatively.

I wonder if he's picked up on something I missed. 'Is something not sitting right with you?'

'I couldn't say. Maybe I imagined it, but... something felt off. I can't narrow it down, unfortunately.'

I make a mental note of my partner's words. I have learned to trust his instinct when it comes to interrogating people. I know I can't always see what he can hear.

'We're back to square one, though,' I say as we near the Underground's entrance.

'I think that our theory is correct and that it all began in that church,' Egan says, reaching for the stair railing and holding on tight before taking the steps down. I mumble my agreement as I follow him.

There are many Londoners already waiting on the platform, and signs announce the next train as being fifteen minutes late.

'What a mess,' I grumble in desperation as I try to find a quiet corner for us to stand as we wait. I crane my neck to look left and right; the entire length of the platform is full of people. '*Porca vacca*,' I curse sotto voce. 'There's no way all of us will be able to fit in on the next train.'

Yet we have no choice but to try, as I have no idea when the next one will come — if there even is a next one. 'Stupid weather,' I mutter out loud, and the woman standing next to us turns to face us.

She's the old nanny type, with a fluffy pink snow hat and one of those pocket dogs held tight in her arms. 'It's only going to get worse,' she whispers confidingly. 'Heard it on the radio before we left home. I'm telling you, there'll be more snow before the day is over.'

I groan at her words and try to make my way to the end of the platform without losing Egan en route.

When the train arrives, I grab a fistful of my friend's coat and drag him along as I squeeze through the crowd. People push and pull, all desperate to get in. The few passengers trying to get out of the train have a hard time cutting through the masses. Curses float around us, and I get elbowed in the ribs at some point. I don't let that deter me, and keep a firm grip on Egan.

We manage to get in before the doors close and, unsurprisingly, find no free seats. I push forward in the car until we're standing near one of the security bars. I indicate its position to Egan, and both of his hands reach out for it.

'Are you okay?' I ask him, sneaking a hand forward to hold on to the bar as well.

'Peachy,' he replies with a tight expression that I can't quite read. It's a mixture of scared, hurt and thoroughly pissed off.

I'm about to reply when the train takes a sharp turn, and all of the passengers are jolted from one side to the other. The man standing behind me bumps into my back with force.

'Sorry, miss,' he says, after righting himself.

I shrug in a what-can-you-do gesture, looking around at the congealed mass of snow hats and scarves.

'Hey, Ash,' I say, raising my voice a little to be heard over the crowd, 'I just realised something.'

'What?' he asks with a hopeful smile. 'That you can borrow your mother's car for the remainder of the winter?'

I chuckle. 'That wouldn't help us much; it's worse on the streets. Lots of car accidents, and some streets are closed because they're covered in snow. There are traffic jams everywhere.'

'Is there a point to your exposé, or are you just trying to work out the worst possible slogan to use for London's next tourism campaign?'

'My exposé was the point,' I say dryly. 'Ash, if we're having such a hard time going from one place to the other, it must be the same for our killer. If he has a car, his itineraries are limited and time-consuming. Sure, he could take the Tube like us and apparently the rest of London, but not with his victim or any of the gear he needs to set up his next stage.'

Egan nods. 'His movements are limited. Weather is going to influence him when it comes to choosing his next crime scene.'

'And you heard that old woman; it's only going to get worse.'

9

Back in the warmth of my flat, Egan and I sit pondering a large map of London spread over the coffee table while we dig into boxes of Chinese takeaway we bought on the way back. Everything was cold by the time we got to the flat, and we had to nuke it in the microwave.

I circle in black East London and mark a cross over the Church of the Living God. Then I cross the place where Carlie was found. 'If we keep to our assumption that the church is in the middle of his comfort zone, and we factor in the weather,' I take a red sharpie and draw a circle around the church, 'I'd say we're looking at a one-mile radius, two at most.'

'It narrows it down,' Egan agrees. 'Is Whitechapel in your circle?'

I look down and nod. 'Partly, yes, but I doubt he'd take Isabella to her ballet company. It's the first place we'd expect him to go. He has to know the Met will be looking for him there.'

Egan inclines his head to the side, a thoughtful expression on his face. 'No, he would prefer somewhere more isolated, quieter. He needs time to stage his tableau, to perfect his scene.'

'So, an abandoned building or warehouse, with no nearby neighbours to complain about the noise.' I look down helplessly at the map.

'But something that has to do with dancing,' Egan points out.

A thought strikes me. 'Can your friend, Charles, help us?'

'I'll give him a ring,' Egan nods, before standing up to retrieve his phone.

'Who is he, anyway?' I ask, curious.

'He's a librarian; we went to college together. He always knows how to get the Braille books I want.'

I raise an eyebrow in curiosity at the revelation that the two met in their youth. 'I hope I'll get to meet him one day.' I'm sure he must have a lot of interesting stories about my friend's rebellious teenage years.

Egan relays to the librarian the location criteria we're looking for, and Charles comes through within the hour. He finds two potential buildings within the two-mile perimeter. The first, an abandoned opera building that had once been in action some twenty years ago before becoming a cinema — popular a few years back, but now only shows peculiar black-and-white features that attract little to no one. The second building is an opera house, still functional although closed for Christmas. After a short debate, we set out for the cinema.

The air is cold as we make our way to Whitechapel Station and from there continue on foot. At least the snow seems to have stopped for now. Dark, heavy clouds hang low in the sky, and little sunlight manages to make it through. Although it's only four in the afternoon, it looks as though night has already started to fall.

The cinema sits at the end of a dark alley, past a shady garage and what seems to be an abandoned textile factory. The alley is narrow, and the tall, dark stone walls have a looming quality to them. They are covered in graffiti. There's your usual teenage nonsense and some more radical statements. I even catch sight of symbols that are gang signs.

The cinema looks old. Its façade is faded and cracked; clearly, it would require more than a simple paint job to make it appealing again. I doubt many people would venture here past curfew; I know I wouldn't.

'We're here,' I say, stopping near the entrance. 'Closed until 2nd January,' I read off a sign taped to the door with adhesive. I try the doorknob anyway, but find it locked.

'Do you see any lights?' Egan asks me.

I give the place a quick once-over. 'No; no sign of life.' The street is quiet and deserted. And yet...

'There are recent prints in the snow,' I grab Egan's arm and backtrack our steps until we get to the corner of the building. I find a small alleyway I had overlooked. 'The trail goes that way,' I continue, and Egan follows me. 'There's a small door here I didn't spot before.'

This time, the door opens when I press the handle. It leads to a dim corridor, and we walk down as quietly as we can. Egan remains close to me, but a little behind, trusting me to take the lead and protect him should the need arise.

We walk through an empty, dimly-lit cafeteria, and continue forward. I'm about to comment on the unsanitary state of the popcorn machine when Egan's grasp on my arm tightens.

I freeze and turn back to him. 'What is it?' I ask in a low whisper.

'Screams,' he rushes, taking a step forward, urging me to get moving again. 'We have to hurry — that way.'

'Stay behind me,' I order as I start walking again, faster this time. With my free hand, I reach for my phone, ready to speed-dial Stenson if need be.

There are stairs at the end of the cafeteria, and we climb them, as per Egan's instruction; I can't hear a thing, but I trust him.

We climb quickly, and by the time we reach the next floor, I can hear them too — shrill, distraught female screams. I hurry forward, hoping we won't be too late for Isabella. I push open the first door I find and stop dead in my tracks at the sight.

There's a man with a knife in his hand and a wild look on his face. He looks feverish, sick even. He seems relentless in the pursuit of the blonde woman he's after, and she screams as she tries to run away from him. Gravel creeks under her bare feet as she runs down the driveway of some posh house. She continues to run through a field and only stops when she arrives at the top of a cliff. The man follows her, of course, and he has her cornered now. The slim, busty blonde woman turns back to face the camera, her silky nightgown blowing in the air. 'Please, let me live,' she whispers as the camera zooms in on her frightened face.

'It's just a film,' I say, even though I suppose Egan has guessed as much by now.

The room is empty, and I wonder who would play a film to

no one; it's probably a test run, part of some maintenance operation.

'We should get out of here before someone sees us,' I mutter, turning on my heel. I hear the blonde woman scream behind us and suppose her attacker is still advancing. I bet the images alternate between close-ups of the blade and the damsel in distress's cleavage.

'We need to hurry to the second address,' I say as we cross the cafeteria again.

10

We make it back to the main road and turn left to go to the opera house. There's little to no life on the streets. On Cavell Street, we pass by an old man hurriedly walking his dog. His thin frame is ensconced in warm layers and faux-fur. A brave cabbie stops by a house on Raven Row. The young woman who exits the black cab hurries to her flat. She's under-dressed, sporting what looks to be a short black dress under a thick coat. She's wearing heels, and she nearly falls over as she climbs her icy steps.

I try to make out street signs and house numbers and lead us through the rapidly falling night. Egan hears the music before I do. He freezes in his step and goes rigid on the pavement. I stop and turn back to look at him, at his face bathed in the yellow light of a nearby streetlamp. The expression he sports is one I've never seen before, and I can't quite decipher it. I've seen him scared, angry, sad; but this is new, and it makes my blood run colder than the weather.

'Ash?' I call out to him, taking a hurried step in his direction. 'What is it?'

His lips part in answer, but no sound comes. Instead, he takes a step forward, then another. I watch him go, bemused and worried.

He passes me and keeps walking forward. Thankfully, he keeps going in a straight line and remains on the pavement.

Stop staring and start walking, I instruct myself, catching up with him. That's when I hear it. The music. It's faint, in the distance, but it drifts to us, carried on the cold wind.

I look around, but have no idea where it could be coming from. There's an empty car park to our right, rows of industrial buildings on our left; they're all closed for the night.

We keep walking and, in the distance, a tall red-brick building appears. There's a large entrance, and two columns carved in stone. The opera house must have been majestic back in the day, but now it looks decrepit and old. Its windows are either tarnished or covered in rudimentary planks of wood. There's moss growing between the bricks in the walls, and assorted advertising posters taped to the columns. As we stand in front of the entrance, I realise the music comes from somewhere inside. This place should also be closed for the Christmas Holidays, and I wonder if this, too, will be a waste of our time.

'Stay here,' I instruct Egan as I climb the steps. No one has cleaned the snow off, and I struggle to get to the door. I try it and find it locked.

I walk back down, follow the length of the building, come back to the front and then try the other side. This time, there are no visible prints to be seen.

Egan is still poised in front of the entrance when I return.

'Found a broken window on the east side. I think I can squeeze in that way,' I tell him.

It seems to shake him up a little, and his vacant expression lifts. 'I'm coming with you.'

I halt him with a palm on his chest. 'Ash, are you okay?'

'I'm fine; it's nothing. Show me the way.' This is a tone I'm familiar with. It's the tone that says he won't change his mind, and I better do as he says. He pushes my hand off. 'Lead the way.'

I grumble but grab his arm nevertheless. Getting the both of us inside is difficult and, to my dismay, noisy. Once we're in, I reach for my phone and activate the flashlight function. It bathes the room in a harsh white light. My gaze settles on a large coat rack, rusty with lack of use. Behind it, I see mirrors and chairs covered in dust. 'I think this may have been a dressing room,' I say, sotto voce.

'The music's coming from that way,' Egan says, pointing to the left.

I move to stand in front of him, offer him my left arm to hold and take slow, quiet steps in the direction he indicated.

We trail down a corridor, climb some steps and arrive in the reception hall. I can hear the music is clearly now, but I can't pinpoint its origin; it feels as if it's all around us.

'Can you tell where it's coming from?' I ask my partner.

He immediately points. 'This way.'

I trust his hearing and creep the way he's indicated until we reach a large wooden door. I turn my lamp off, slowly push the door open and peer inside to find we're in the heart of the opera house now. The path ahead leads us through rows of dusty and sometimes broken seats, all the way to the elevated main stage.

Two projectors are turned on, their lights cast straight at the centre of the stage. I pocket my phone, having no need for the additional light anymore.

Although I wish I could turn my back on this stage — run far, far away from here, to a place where I could pretend I've never been here, never seen the sickening image displayed in front of me — I can't. I force myself to swallow around the lump growing in my throat and start walking down the central aisle that leads up to the stage and the macabre tableau that has been erected there.

Isabella's features get easier to distinguish as we draw closer. She's unscathed but looks thinner than on the photographs I have seen. She is dressed in a ballet dancer's costume: nude tights, a pearl-white leotard, pale rose pointe shoes and a matching skirt. Her posture is full of grace, the bow of her arms a perfect oval. Light falls on her at a faultless angle, shimmering on her pale skin. Even her dark hair seems to glisten in the light as it cascades down her slender shoulders.

On the whole, the scene is elegant, much like a painting. It leaves spectators envious of the dancer's grace and beauty. It catches your breath and holds your interest. It's mesmerising...

... until your eyes take in the minor details that don't add up.

The awe is quick to desert you once you take in the nylon rope cutting deep into the dancer's wrists; the twin set of ropes, bound just above her hands, obviously intended to support all of the woman's weight, are too much for her pale skin to handle. The splendour rapidly deserts the tableau once the onlooker notices the torn skin and the scarlet droplets running along the young woman's bare arms. The crude black stitches used to keep her eyelids open detract from the beauty of her face. And once you really pay attention, it becomes evident that her alabaster skin is too pale to be considered healthy.

Yes, once taken in its entirety, this tableau leaves you feeling one thing: deep and wretched disgust.

I feel my stomach churn, and bile rise up. I hastily take a step to the side before I throw up. Egan is by my side in a second, and I have to hold him off at arm's length to stop him from stepping into what used to be my lunch.

I dry-heave a few times before I manage to get my breathing in check.

'Isabella...' Egan's voice is toneless. 'She's dead.'

It wasn't a question, but I answer anyway. 'Yes. We're too late.'

'Same as the others,' Egan states. Once again, it was not a question.

'Yes. How'd you know?'

'The smells and,' he waves a hand about, 'you told me the rest.'

'*Vaffanculo!*' I curse loudly before taking a careful step to the side. When I look up at my partner, I'm met with a cold face on which not a single feeling can be deciphered through the ice. He's wearing the thickest of his masks. How could he look so unaffected? I'm tempted to rip off his glasses to see if his eyes hold any kind of feeling, or if they're as dead as Isabella's.

Isabella. I turn and face the ballerina again. I fight the urge to rush to the stage, cut those nylon ropes and free the poor girl from this twisted, insulting macabre pose. I refrain, knowing it would compromise the official investigation.

Music keeps playing around us, that same classical sorrowful tune. I look about to see if I can find out how to turn it off. 'Is this from *Giselle*, too?' I ask Egan, more to distract myself than out of curiosity.

His voice is as toneless as before, as he replies, 'No, it's not.'

There's a black cable running from one of the speakers; I follow it, thinking it may lead to the soundboard or something. It leads me straight to an electricity socket. Without thinking twice, I yank the cable. It does the job, and the room falls silent. When I turn on my heels to face the room again, I find Egan gone.

Worry grips me as I rush back to the place where I'd last seen him. 'Ash?'

There's no reply, and I can't help but imagine the worst. Could the killer be here? Has he taken my friend? Has he... I look about wildly, but can't find anything.

A noise distracts me in the distance; it sounded like a door closing. I head off in pursuit, rushing up the row of seats, running through the door and on through the main hall. There, I find the front door half open. It was locked before, I remember.

In lieu of a small handle, this side of the door has a large horizontal bar like an emergency door, I realise; push it, and you're free. No one could have come in, but someone could have gone out. I dash forward, push the door open and stop short on the entrance steps. The sight I find there catches me off guard.

It turns out my friend's all right after all. Egan is walking away, safe and sound, his white cane in hand. I see him hobbling down the street. He is slipping and sliding on the slick ice and snow. I call out his name, but he doesn't stop.

I run after him, mindful of the treacherous snow-covered street under my boots. Once at his level, I catch him by the arm and force him to stop and face me. 'Where on earth are you going?' I ask, out of breath.

'Leave me be,' he snaps. His voice is as cold as the air around us.

'Ash, we can't leave. We have to wait for the Met to arrive and then give our statements.'

He shakes himself free of my grasp. 'Then *you* stay.'

I look at the street ahead, see the snow and the ice, and try to reason with him. 'You can't go home on your own; you'll break your neck.'

My words seem to anger him more. 'I don't need your help getting home, Alexandra. I didn't go blind yesterday. This isn't my first winter.'

The use of my full name causes my eyebrow to rise. Egan never calls me Alexandra unless he's mad at me. For the life of me, I can't think what it is I've done wrong this time.

'Leave me alone!' he spits again, then turns his back on me and takes a step away. I bite my lip, hard enough to draw blood, to stop myself from saying something stupid.

I stare at my partner as he rushes away, torn between following him to make sure he doesn't do anything stupid or get hurt and calling in the crime scene as I know I'm supposed to do. The image of Isabella's mangled body is fresh in my mind, and I know the sooner the police arrive, the sooner the ugly nylon ropes will be cut and she will be removed from that horrible stage. Duty wins, and I let Egan go.

With the coppery taste of blood fresh in my mouth, I call Stenson and tell him to get here double-quick.

11

I meet up with Stenson when he and his team arrive, and give him a brief summary of what we found. Officers close off the area and begin their investigation. A medical examiner is brought in, and what the short silver-haired man discovers breaks my heart.

By combining body temperature, room temperature, and the nature of the wounds, he's able to ascertain that Egan and I were only a few hours late. A few hours, no more. A full autopsy should allow him to narrow it down, but the estimate is quite enough to turn my stomach upside-down all over again.

Tears spring to my eyes and I move to the nearest seat. '*Porca vacca,*' I mutter in my hands. 'If we hadn't wasted our time with the cinema, if we'd come here sooner, just a few hours earlier...'

The notion of time is at the forefront of my mind; it eclipses everything else as I focus on it. Tick-tock; too little, too late.

I feel a hand on my knee and open my eyes to find Stenson crouched in front of me. 'It's not your fault, Alex,' he says, in a voice one would use with a frightened child. 'You couldn't have known.'

'We were a hair's breadth away from saving her, Matthew,' I say in a broken tone. 'Don't you dare tell me it's not my fault.'

A hair's breadth. A handful of minutes. Tick-tock. I can't help but retrace our steps in my mind. 'What if I'd woken up earlier this morning? What if we'd skipped lunch? What if we hadn't stopped for that tea break? What if...?'

'Alexandra, don't!' Stenson reaches for my hands.

The what-ifs won't stop coming. Tears fall from my eyes, but I can't be bothered to do anything about it. What if I'm not cut out for this job, after all? 'We were on a missing person case, and we took breaks. Who does that? Jokes, laughs, a phone call to Mum and stopping at a shop for a chocolate bar.' My eyes are drawn to the medical examiner as he finishes writing his notes. Isabella's body is right beside him. The ballerina has taken her final bow; she lies motionless, under a white sheet now.

I feel my heart being crushed in my chest as I think of her mother. I will have to break the news to her. How does one do that?

'Saying hello to one of Ash's neighbours as he took out his rubbish and walking down to the station at a leisurely pace. Damn it; if we'd hurried, we might have caught an earlier train.'

My breath seems to clog in my windpipe, unable to pass through the lump that has settled there. My vision darkens; everything becomes blurry and obscured.

I'm half-aware of Stenson's arms around me, grabbing and

pulling. It feels as if I'm on my feet a moment later, dragged and carried out of the room. My brain is muddled, slowed down by the air deprivation. I'm unable to inhale properly. White spots appear all around me: tiny, bright, white lights. They grow bigger and bigger as the seconds tick away, and everything becomes whiter. Pristine white, like the snow that blankets the City. Pristine white, like the sheet that covers Isabella's body.

Is this what death is like? Cold and white?

A sharp, tingling sensation brings me back to my senses. Reflexively, I take in a deep breath of air — cold, fresh air, I notice. As my vision returns, I realise that I'm outside, sitting on a bench near the building's entrance.

My left cheek throbs and I bring a hand up to massage it. 'Did you just slap me?'

Stenson gives me a coy smile, nodding. 'It was all I could think of.'

'Is that what they teach you in police school?' I ask, massaging the tender flesh.

He holds up both hands in surrender. 'Hey, it worked!'

I must admit it did. 'Sorry, about... that.' I wave a hand about, unsure of what *that* was. Shock, probably.

I look back at the front door and swallow the bile back down. 'Please, Matthew, tell me that I will never have to go back in there.'

'I promise you; you won't.' He sits down next to me. 'I'm so sorry you had to see that; it would've been difficult to stomach even for the most seasoned detective.'

'What do they teach you about crime scenes in police school?' I ask, curious.

Stenson sighs, bringing his hands together as he leans forward. 'They tell us it will get easier with time.'

'And does it?'

A sour smile crosses my friend's thin lips as he shakes his head. 'No, it never does. It's not all crap, though. There is one thing they got right.'

I turn a little to face him and motion for him to continue.

'It wasn't your fault, Alex. You did your job, you tried.' He reaches for my hands, wraps warm fingers around mine. 'You did your best, and you know it. You can never blame yourself if you did your best. We are not gods; we can't save everyone – it's not in our power. Our job is not over; our task remains the same – find whoever did this, and bring him to justice.'

There is some truth to those words, I know, but it's not enough to take the guilt away.

Someone calls out Stenson's name in the distance. He looks up and makes a just-a-minute gesture.

When I look in the same direction, I see a plump duffle coat on legs that looks like DI Langford, waiting impatiently. I should laugh at the sight, but can't muster the energy.

'They need me back inside,' Stenson says before calling out to one of the constables patrolling the area. 'I'll ask someone to drive you home.'

'No. I have another stop to make first.' I stand, straighten my back. 'My client, Isabella's mother. I have to tell her; I owe her that much.'

Stenson's face saddens at my words. 'You can't; it's our job. She has to come and identify the body. There's a procedure to follow, Alex.'

'Sorry, yeah... you're right.' I knew that, of course, I knew that. 'I failed her. God, I failed her.'

'You did your job. We both did,' Stenson says, guiding me towards the young policewoman who had just joined us. 'Take her back to her place, please,' he instructs.

I turn back to face him, dazed, and not quite comprehending why he's so stern with me. 'Matthew?'

'You need to go home and get some sleep. I'll see you tomorrow.' He nods to the constable again. 'Take her home, nowhere else.'

'Yes, DS Stenson,' the woman answers, motioning to her nearby police car.

I follow her, feeling deflated and incompetent.

I reach the car and get in without a fuss. The constable smiles pleasantly as she asks for my address. I give her Egan's instead of mine. Seemingly pleased, she drives into the night. She must only be a year or two older than me, and she attempts some small-talk as she turns into Whitechapel Road. She brings up the weather, of all things. I don't feel like talking and turn to stare out of the window. It takes nearly a mile for my driver to get the message and give up on the chitchat.

When she drops me in front of Egan's building, I thank her politely. I make a good show of entering the building as if I own the place. I hear the police car depart, once the front door has closed behind me.

Egan doesn't open when I knock on his door. I knock again and again, louder each time. 'I know you're in there!' I tell the dark-brown door. 'I'm not going away until we've talked.'

There's no answer, and I kick the door with the tip of my

boot. 'You know me, Ash. I can be stubborn when I want to, so you'd better let me in before I make a scene.'

I listen at the door but can't hear anything, although I'm certain he's home. Where else could he be, really? His home is his sanctum; he always retreats there when he needs to feel safe.

I reach for my phone and dial his number. He won't be able to pretend he's not here once I've heard the familiar ringtone. I listen to the rings in my ear: one, two, three, four, and voicemail. I end the call with a frown; there wasn't a sound from the flat.

'*Porca vacca*, Ash.' That same feeling of dread I felt earlier rises up in me again. 'Where on earth are you?'

I try to call him again as I jog back down the stairs. I zip my duffle coat back up and push my hands deep in my pockets, realising I've lost my gloves at some point tonight.

Worry grips me as I find myself back on the pavement looking left and right. I knew this was a bad idea; I should never have let him go home alone. I should have gone with him. I could have called in the scene on the way back and dropped by New Scotland Yard tomorrow for a statement.

I curse out loud, unsure which way to go. I last saw Egan walking west. Where would he have gone? 'Think, Lexa, think!'

Nearest Underground station: Whitechapel. Most logical journey: Hammersmith & City line to King's Cross Station and then the Piccadilly line to Russell Square. I turn my head to look south. Russell Square station is just around the corner.

I walk down Herbrand Street at a fast pace, reach the corner and prepare to turn left in Bernard Street. I can almost make out the red-and-blue Underground sign from here. I scan the street but see no sign of Egan.

I'm torn; his words resound in my ears, echoes of our last

conversation. Not his first winter. He'd been right; he's been blind for a long time, and he knows how to get around London on his own. It was a pretty straightforward trip. He was mere streets away from the first Tube station, and it was all familiar territory. I look down at my watch, and know with certainty that if he'd taken the straight road home, he should be here already.

'Then why the hell are you not at home?' I mutter at the dark street ahead.

I take my phone out and redial his number, but to no avail.

'Think, Lexa. Think.' Where else could he have gone?

Luigi's? Too much noise and life for how Egan must be feeling right now. The university? A good fit, but it's closed at this time of the day, and he knows it. My place? I doubt it; he made it clear he didn't want to see me. I need to think of more places. Somewhere he likes, somewhere that could fit his current state of mind. Empty, quiet, cold. In the end, I'm left with only one guess.

I push both hands in my pockets again, turn on my heels and walk down Bernard Street in the opposite direction. Five minutes later, I'm at the North East entrance of Russell Square Park. The place is eerily quiet under the night sky. The immaculate snow which blankets the ground and coats the nearby trees gives a sort of timeless feeling to the scene.

I step forward, the snow crunching under my boots. A little further into the park, I find Egan sitting on a bench. His cane is resting limply in his gloved fingers. He is so motionless he could be mistaken for a statue.

'You're going to catch a cold if you stay out here all night,' I say, to let him know I'm the one approaching, although I'm pretty sure he'll have already guessed it was me.

He offers me no acknowledgment.

'I mean it, Ash. It must be below zero already. You're going to catch your death if you stay here.'

I crouch in front of him and am relieved when I see his breath turning into fog every time he exhales. This is the only indication he's alive, not a statue — just a man with a face carved in ice.

On closer inspection, I note the pallor of his skin, and the light-blue tinge to his lips makes up my mind.

'All right.' I reach for the lapel of his coat. 'Enough is enough. Come on; we're going home.' I yank him upwards, and the motion seems to bring him back to life.

'Let go of me.' He shoves me off, makes a wide arc with his arm until his fist connects with my shoulder, forcing me to take a step back. 'I'm not a child in constant need of your help and attention. I'm not a broken toy that you need to fix.'

I take another step back, reeling from his tone. The rage, the anger beneath his words, they burn like only ice can.

'Leave me alone!' he screams at me before taking a step to the left, then one to the right, seemingly lost. His cane falls to the ground and rolls under the bench when he stands up. He'll never get out of the park without it, and he knows it.

I take a tentative step towards him. 'Ash?'

'Leave me alone!' he roars again.

His tone startles me. I've never seen him so out of sorts; I've never heard him lose his temper. Something deep inside me makes me take a figurative step back, and I listen to him and analyse what is going on with more rationality. I *really* listen, and what I hear, underneath the anger and the hurt, underneath the rage and the pain, is 'don't leave me.'

I take a step forward and another, and wrap both arms around him. He resists for just an instant, before going limp against me.

'Never,' I whisper, in his ear. A distant promise made a long time ago — the words which cemented our friendship. 'I'll never leave you alone.'

.

12

Less than twenty minutes later, I have Egan safely tucked under a thick duvet, three blankets and the comforter. Even though he should be warm by now, he is shivering from the cold. I get him to drink some warm tea, to which I have added two spoonfuls of honey to prevent a sore throat. The bluish undertones are starting to leave his lips. A few minutes later, pink starts to tinge his cheeks again.

'You silly man,' I mutter as I set my empty cup on his bedside table. 'What did you think you were doing?'

My friend offers me no reply — not that I was expecting one.

A look at my watch reveals that it's almost midnight, and I let out a weary sigh, feeling drained and tired to the bone. What a day.

Egan's shivering subdues as the minutes tick away, and he falls asleep. I stand and contemplate dragging my drained body to his settee to have a snooze myself, when Egan's soft voice surprises me.

'I'm sorry,' he says.

I turn back to look at him, wondering if I imagined hearing his voice.

He hasn't moved and still has his eyes closed. As I watch, I see his lips form words again. 'I shouldn't have talked to you like that.'

'It's fine,' I say, standing poised near his bed. 'We both had a lousy day.'

Silence falls on us again, and I wonder what more could be said. I don't think any words can make a day like this one better.

'Thanks for the tea,' Egan says, his words spoken softly and tentatively. He's not talking about the drink. I understand the words for what they are: 'Thank you for being here.'

'Any time,' I say before exiting his bedroom.

I slump on his settee a minute later, only to realise there's no blanket left to keep *me* warm tonight. I'm too tired to mind, and I reach for my coat.

The next morning, I awake to the smell of coffee. I blink my eyes open and find a steaming red mug floating in front of me within easy reach. I blink again, follow the fingers holding the mug, up the length of an arm, then all the way up to a familiar face topped with ginger curls. I smile despite myself at Egan's I-just-got-out-of-bed face, wrinkled t-shirt and sweatpants. I don't often see him in casual clothes, and a look at the large scar that runs from the side of his neck down his collarbone reminds me why he always wears turtlenecks no matter the season.

'Morning,' I mutter, pushing myself up and shrugging off the duffle coat underneath which I slept.

'Good morning, Lexa.'

I reach for the proffered mug and swallow down a large gulp. Egan sits on the coffee table, a mug of his own resting next to him.

'So,' I ask, tentatively, yesterday's event fresh in my mind, 'how are we feeling today?'

The fake smile on Egan's lips is too large to be true. 'I'm fine. Thank you.'

I could give him a free pass, but don't feel like it. Not after the scare he gave me. 'And I'm going to enter some random shop, buy the first scratch card I see and win a million quid.'

My joke has little to no effect on him. He shrugs a shoulder, 'It could happen.'

'Yeah, right — like I could ever be that lucky.' I swallow another gulp of coffee and stretch my back as I try to find a good way to broach the subject in hand. I've never been good at this sort of thing, and today is no exception.

'Ash, I found you pretending to be an ice lolly in a park in the middle of the night. Don't tell me you're fine.'

Egan's mouth quirks downward at the mention of last night's events, and he closes his eyes. He leaves me clueless, as his face loses all traces of emotion.

'What happened?' I ask, keeping my tone gentle.

'Nothing.' A moment passes, then he adds, 'I was just lost in a memory.'

I hate having to push, but he leaves me no choice. 'Which one?'

'Lexa...'

'Tell me, please.'

He reopens his eyes at my plea and tries to find my gaze, or at least that is the impression I get. He misses, of course, but even with him staring to the left of me, I can see the repressed tears in his eyes and the pain amidst the blue flakes of his irises. 'Please, Lexa, drop it.'

It's a good impression of a puppy dog's eyes. It's impossible to fight him when he tries this hard. I change tactics and fall back on what Stenson told me. 'It wasn't our fault. We tried our best.'

Somehow, the words sound less hollow when I use them for someone else's benefit. 'We can't blame ourselves if we did our best.'

Egan nods and sips his coffee. His eyes flicker away in another direction. 'Poor kid,' he mutters. 'Abandoned, with no one coming to rescue her.'

'That isn't true,' I counter. '*We* tried.'

With a shaking hand, he places his mug back on the table and continues as if I hadn't interrupted. 'It's always like that, isn't it? We always die alone in the end.'

I get the distinct feeling we are not talking about Isabella anymore. 'What happened?'

His lips twist in a grim smile as he gives me the patented reply, 'A lot.'

'Damn it, Ash, there is only so much I can do. I can promise to walk by your side, to protect you and be your friend — but you're the only one who can decide to let me in.'

'You're being unfair,' he says.

Frustration rises in me, and my next words are louder than they should have been. 'No. *You're* being unfair. And you know it. Being friends is about sharing things, good and bad alike.'

My tone surprises Egan, and I can see it.

I should apologise and take the words back, but I can't, not after everything that happened yesterday. I suppose somehow we both knew it would come to this; some secrets just cannot be kept forever. 'It's gone on long enough, don't you think?'

I can see in my friend's shoulders the moment he decides to give up; a slight slump forward reveals his intention. It's accompanied by faint tremors in his hands. I feel bad for putting him in such a tight spot, I really do. However, an incident like last night cannot be allowed to happen again. Not in our line of work.

Egan clasps both hands together in his lap before he begins. 'Right after I got my PhD, I took a year off to visit a few places. I went to France, walked the same roads the troopers marched on D-Day. I went to Germany, touched what was left of the wall. I went to Asia, visited Cambodia and Vietnam; you know... places of historical interest.'

I smile, as I try to conjure up a younger version of him, with a backpack on his shoulders and travelling on his lonesome. 'Yeah, I get the idea.'

'My last Asian stop—' he sighs '—well, my last stop altogether, was a small village near Lijiang, in the province of Yunnan in the southwest of the country.'

Lijiang... the word is somehow familiar; a distant memory, fleeting, that I cannot grab.

'I had found a cheap hotel, a four-storey building. Some of the staff spoke a little English,' Egan continues. 'I came back to my room one evening, tired from a long walk around town followed by a visit to the market. It must have been close to five when the walls, floor and ceiling started to shake violently. 7.0

on the Richter scale, I learned later,' he indicates, almost as an afterthought.

There! Lijiang: the earthquake. I remember the name now. I've never felt an earthquake — they're not very common in the UK — but I can imagine how horrible it must be when the whole world starts to shake around you for no apparent reason.

'It took some time for me to fathom what was going on,' Egan continues, his hands still firmly clasped together. 'I couldn't find my cane anywhere; I tried to make it to the door anyway, hoped someone would help me. I heard some people running about, screaming in Chinese. I called for help, but no one stopped for me. I tried as hard as I could to follow in the direction I'd heard them run.

'I had barely made it to the top of the stairs when the first aftershock occurred. It sent me toppling down, and I banged my head hard against the wall.'

I watch as small tremors course through the length of Egan's arms. His fingers remain clasped together, knuckles white under the strain. I force myself to keep silent, not wanting to interrupt his tale, unsure if he will continue if I do so.

'I lay there, dazed for a while. I called for help again, to no avail,' he continues, his tone subdued. 'Eventually, I dragged myself to my feet and tried to walk down the steps. There was another aftershock. I was holding on to the railing, so it had little impact on me, but I heard glass shatter nearby. Windows breaking, I supposed. I heard something ripping and tearing, and then the whole structure of the building yawning loudly as I felt its foundations shift underneath my feet. It was as if the hotel itself was screaming its pain.'

I've seen it many times on the television. Indonesia, Japan, the views were all similar. Buildings turned to mere rubble after cracks along their length brought them down. Entire families made homeless in a matter of minutes, losing everything in a heartbeat.

'There was a third aftershock when I was between the first floor and the ground floor. The staircase collapsed underneath me. I fell forward, tumbled, rolled. I didn't know which way was up anymore. I broke a hand at some point. When the world stopped spinning, I was laying on some rubble, water dripping on me from somewhere above. Everything hurt, every part of me.

'Dust was clogging the air, making it hard to breathe. I could taste the particles of concrete, wood and metal with every intake of air. I called out for help again and again, but there was no one to reply. They'd left me alone.'

I reach out for his hands at the pain I hear in his voice, and wrap my fingers around his. It takes time before he continues.

'I was hurting all over, but I managed to get to my knees. I kept moving forward, towards the exit or so I hoped. I crawled on debris, cutting my palms and knees open until I heard a crack. It came from above; an indistinct sound that I couldn't quite place. I froze as I tried to label it, and a second later, something sharp cut right through me.'

Reflexively, one of his hands flies up to his neck, cradling the side of his throat protectively.

I don't need more explanation to understand where his large, ugly scar comes from. As if that day had not been horrible enough, fate decided he'd have to live with a crude reminder that would force him to wear turtlenecks and scarves for the rest of his life.

'I don't know what it was — glass from a window, a shard from some large mirror? All I know is that it detached itself and fell, and I was in its path. A little bit more to the side, and I'd have lost my head, like King Charles.' He chuckles humourlessly at his bad joke. I can't find the heart to even fake a smile.

'I was bleeding, crying out in pain, calling, begging for help, but no one came. Not a soul. I stayed there for minutes, hours, I don't know. I could feel the blood run down my neck. My hands and knees were on fire. There were splinters, shards of metal everywhere...

'I don't know how, but I managed to haul myself outside. I passed out from blood loss in the street and woke up two days later in a hospital. The doctors told me I was lucky; the injuries would heal, I'd get better. A lot of people died that day, and I wasn't one of them. I could put this behind me; forget it ever happened. But I never did.'

Once I'm sure he's finished his tale, I engulf him in a fierce hug. 'You're not there anymore; nor are you alone anymore. I will always come and find you — you know that.'

'Yeah, you will,' he says. 'You will.' If anything, he sounds surprised at the realisation, as if some grand truth about the mysteries of the universe had been revealed to him.

I smile at him, for him, and force the gesture into my voice. 'You bet I will.'

When he's ready, he lets me go and collects himself. I see him wipe tears from his eyes as I reach for my discarded coffee mug, but I don't mention it.

'There was a song,' he says. 'When I was in that lobby, bleeding out.'

'What song?' I ask.

'I don't know the title, I never knew, never wanted to find out.'

Understanding dawns on me. 'The same song playing when we arrived at the opera house yesterday?'

Egan nods. 'When I heard it, it brought everything back.' He swallows. 'Now more than ever, I hope never to hear it again.'

13

Towards the end of the morning, I draw up the courage to dial Mrs Doughton's number. I know I'm not supposed to talk to her, but I have to say something to the poor woman. She picks up on the fourth ring and enunciates her name with difficulty. I don't need Egan's super-hearing to know there are tears in her voice.

'Mrs Doughton, this is Alexandra Neve,' I start then stop, unsure what to say next.

I had prepared a speech in my head, but now that I'm on the phone with Isabella's mother, thoughts are hard to form. 'I—I wanted to call... to say how sorry I am.'

I swallow, search for the right words, but they seem determined to elude me. 'I—we... we wish this could have ended differently. I... we're terribly sorry for your loss.'

'The police told me you were the ones who found her?' she asks.

I swallow as images from the night prior resurface. 'Yes, we did.'

'Thank you, Ms Neve,' Mrs Doughton says, her voice a little stronger now.

Her words surprise me. I do not feel worthy of her gratitude and mumble something unintelligible in reply.

'I'm sorry, but I have to go,' Mrs Doughton cuts into my mumbles. 'I'll prepare your cheque later today, and post it to you.'

Money couldn't be further from my mind right now, and my answer is once more barely coherent. 'Mrs Doughton, I ... huh ... I don't—'

'Four hundred a day, plus expenses was it?' she continues, as if I hadn't spoken.

I give her a faint affirmative hum. 'There weren't any expenses.'

'Fine. You'll have the cheque tomorrow. Thank you for calling,' she says, before ending the call.

'That's not why I called,' I say to the disconnected beeping line. I remain perched on the edge of the settee, phone in hand, for several minutes. It is the shrill sound of the doorbell that gets me back on my feet.

'I'll get it,' I call out, already stepping into the corridor. Egan still hasn't come out of his bedroom.

Our visitor is none other than Detective Sergeant Matthew Stenson of the Metropolitan Police. He looks tired, and I surmise he hasn't slept at all last night.

'Hey.' I smile at him as I step aside.

'Good morning,' he replies, lifting up a white bag with a red Chinese logo on it. 'Hope you haven't had lunch yet.'

It smells delicious, and my empty stomach growls in anticipation. 'We were just about to go out for lunch.'

I have just finished laying the table when Egan joins us, light beige turtleneck on, hair perfectly combed. I can't help but stare for a second or two at his neck, now that I know the truth behind the scar that hides underneath the woollen material.

'Do I detect an Asian aroma in the air?' he asks.

'Matthew was nice enough to bring us some food,' I reply, looking away.

Egan nods his appreciation. 'That's very kind.'

'I also wanted to give you a rundown of the investigation. I thought you two would be interested,' he says, sitting down.

I dig into the Cantonese rice wolfishly. 'What have you found?'

'The post-mortem on Isabella is being carried out as we speak. Forensics swiped the scene with a fine-tooth comb all night.'

'And?' Egan asks, hopeful.

'Nothing. Not a single fingerprint or hair, or—' Stenson makes an exasperated all-encompassing gesture with his chopstick '—anything else.'

'How is it even possible?' I ask.

'The killer must be very careful and well informed. He knows police procedures and which mistakes to avoid.'

'That doesn't help us much.' I snort. 'Anyone who's ever watched CSI knows to wear gloves when killing someone.'

'There was one noteworthy fact, though,' Stenson replies, ignoring my weak joke. 'We think the killer left the crime scene by using an abandoned Underground tunnel.'

That surprises me. 'How did you work that out?'

'The snow helped us with that one. The only footprints visible in the snow when we arrived were yours and Egan's.' Stenson sends a pointed look my way.

The reproachful gaze has little effect on me, and I offer him a polite smile in return. 'It had just stopped snowing when we left the flat yesterday afternoon, and it only started snowing again late last night,' I recall. 'The killer could have left as snow was falling?'

'No. The ME narrowed down the time of death...' Stenson seems to hesitate, before continuing. 'Thirty minutes — an hour max — before you two arrived. Way after it stopped snowing.'

An hour. There's a hard pill to swallow. Out of the corner of my eye, I note that Egan does the same maths as I did. Damn it, if we hadn't gone to the cinema first... I reach for his arm under the table and wrap a comforting hand around his wrist.

'The killer's prints should have been visible in the snow,' Stenson continues. 'That bugged us until Langford found a disused maintenance shaft that leads to an old Tube line.'

I can't help but roll my eyes at the mention of Stenson's ill-tempered superior. I refrain from any crude comment, due to his usefulness for once.

'We've contacted Transport for London to get some detailed maps and authorisations to send men down there.'

'Utility shafts and old Tube lines,' Egan muses, apparently deep in thought. 'I wonder...'

I turn to him, waiting to see where his line of thought will lead us.

He reaches a hand up to scratch his chin. 'He may have left that way, but I doubt he brought Isabella to the Opera house using the tunnels.'

'Why not?' I ask.

'I would love to see you climb a ladder with someone unconscious on your back... if only I wasn't blind,' he says with his usual dry humour.

'Yeah, right. So he has a car to transport the victims, and he uses the Underground for hasty exits.'

'Our assumption as well.' Stenson says, more level-headed.

'Right. Have you got any other leads we could follow?' I demand.

Stenson's eyes shoot my way.

I frown in response. 'What?'

He seems unsure how to respond, and settles for a hesitant, 'I thought you would consider your job to be done now.'

Egan beats me to the reply. 'We'll be done when the killer is caught. Helping you to find him is the least we can do.'

Stenson must have expected this answer because his face registers no surprise; his sour look doesn't lift either.

'What is it, Matthew?' I demand, looking him squarely in the eye.

'Langford almost had a fit when he found out you called in the crime scene.'

I remember the murderous gaze the DI threw my way when he and Stenson arrived. Normally I'd have replied in kind, but I was too shaken.

'From now on, he wants you as far away as can be,' the sergeant continues. 'He convinced the Chief Superintendent it should be so, and he agreed.'

'What has Saunders got to do with any of this?' I question, remembering the chief superintendent, whom I met earlier this year.

DCS Saunders, Stenson's boss's boss, is a tall, dark-haired man in his mid-forties, with control-freak tendencies that border on obsessive–compulsive disorder.

'This is a high-profile case, Alex. Like any other serial killer case, it has us all on our toes.'

'I don't get why Saunders wouldn't want all the help he can get to tie this case up ASAP.'

We finish our lunch in silence, and as Stenson prepares to take his leave, I say my goodbyes to Egan and accompany the detective outside. It is time for me to go home and face my mother. She texted me several times to see what I was up to and if I'd forgotten what time of year it was. Apparently, I sort of did; it was hard to reconcile Christmas and baubles with a murder investigation. I tried telling her that I had better things to do, but it was a lost cause. Some traditions, it would seem, must be upheld no matter the circumstances.

'Do you need a lift?' Stenson asks as we get outside.

I turn back to face him with a smile. 'No, I'm good. I have a few stops to make on the way.'

He smiles at me, a little awkwardly — I suppose I must look similar as I wait for him to reply. I think of asking him out for a drink sometime... but this doesn't feel like the right time.

He scratches at the back of his neck, the motion endearing. 'So, um...'

My smile stays plastered on. 'Yeah?'

He returns it, 'I... um...'

'Thanks for the food,' I blurt out.

'Sure, no problem.' He passes a hand through his dark curls, apparently content I've saved him from having to come up with something to say. 'Are you okay?'

'I'm fine,' I shrug. 'Considering...'

'Yeah, me too.' He pauses, looks away for an instant. 'It's never easy.'

I look to the side too. 'Yeah.'

'You can call me, you know... if you need someone to talk to.'

'Thanks,' I say, not looking at him.

The silence stretches out, and I turn back to face him again. I catch him watching me with a sad, forlorn expression. I soldier on; force my lips to stretch into something that resembles a smile. 'I'll be okay. Don't worry.'

He nods, seemingly relieved. 'I'll better get going, then, yeah? I'll call you when I have news.'

With that, he offers me a last goodbye wave, and he turns to walk up to his car. I take the Tube north, stopping en route for a bit of Christmas shopping, and head back home.

The scent of pine needles assaults me when I open the door to my flat. Sure enough, a large Christmas tree stands in the corner of our tiny living room. My mother has pulled out all the decoration boxes and put them on the coffee table and the settee; she hasn't started to decorate yet though.

'Ah, there you are!' she says, coming out of the kitchen with — I sigh at the sight — mistletoe hanging on a red ribbon. 'Have you had lunch?'

'Yes, we ate at Egan's,' I reply, taking off my coat and stepping out of my snow boots.

'Everything okay?' my mother asks. 'Is your case going well?'

I don't see the point in lying to her. Saunders may be able to keep the serial killer side of the story out of the press, but there's no way he can make a murder disappear. Isabella's death will soon be all over the papers. 'We found her,' I say, in a monotone voice. 'Not soon enough, though.'

'Oh, my dear girl.' My mother drops the mistletoe on the back of the settee and engulfs me in a hug. 'I'm so sorry.'

I let her hug me for a minute, and then work myself out of her embrace.

'This job...' she starts.

I raise a palm. 'Not now, Mum.' We've had this discussion before time and time again, and I'm too tired for an encore. 'I'm not changing my mind; I *am* a private investigator. Now, do you want help with the tree or not?'

She nods and makes a visible effort to change the subject. 'Garlands or baubles?'

We split the tasks, argue for a good ten minutes over which colour we're going to use this year, and decide to only use silver. I handle the tinsel, and my mother does the rest, while Barbra Streisand's Christmas Album plays on a nearby radio.

I'm trying to place a small garland around the top of the tree when my phone rings. Holding the garland up with one hand, I reach in my pocket for my phone. As I look at the caller ID, I'm surprised to discover Egan's name.

I flip the phone open, one-handed. 'Hey.'

'Good evening, Lexa dear,' he says, sounding as pompous as can be.

'Yo, wazup?' I demand with a smile, holding the garland.

'Really?' he asks. 'That's the best you can do?' He tsk-tsks me before continuing. 'I had an interesting revelation this evening.'

I flick my free hand until the stupid garland catches on the needles. 'Have you decided to dress up as Santa for Christmas?'

'About the case.' Egan says, ignoring my comment.

'Hold on,' I turn to my mum, mouth the word *work* and relocate to my bedroom-cum-office, closing the door behind me. 'All right, I'm listening.'

'Did you know my friend Charles has a passion, a hobby of sorts, for trains?'

'Trains?' I echo.

'Yes, trains, as in all kinds of vehicles that follow rails, including those that travel beneath our very feet.'

I know what's coming, and reach for my bag and start tossing a few things in it. 'A passion, you said?'

Egan hums lightly. 'He has, I believe, the largest collection of documents on the London Underground, from its creation until today. From the 19th century to the 21st.'

I cross the living room, shrug my coat back on and reach for the boots. 'Including maps, I suppose?'

'Evidently,' Egan says smugly.

'Evidently. I'll come pick you up in about thirty minutes. How does that sound?'

'I'll be ready.'

We hang up, and I tie my scarf around my neck.

'Going out, I presume?' my mother asks, both hands on her hips and a reproachful gaze fixed on me. The I'm-cross-with-you vibe is somewhat diminished by the sparkling silver garland hanging around her neck.

'It's for work,' I reply with my best I'm-sorry smile.

'But it's almost eight,' she says, reproachful gaze not wavering. 'It's dark outside.'

I walk past her and zip up my coat. 'I'm a big girl, Mum; I can stay up late now.'

'But it's our Christmas tree,' she counters. 'We always decorate it together. It's tradition.'

I offer her another I'm-sorry smile. 'I'm sure you'll manage without me. Look, Mum, I have to go. It's important.'

She scoffs, 'More important than your mother, I see.'

I cringe at the low blow, take a step towards her and reach for her hands. 'He killed three women, and he may already have kidnapped his fourth victim. Think about that for a minute. If it were me, if someone had taken *me*... wouldn't you want people to do everything they can to bring me home?'

My words have the desired effect, and my mother's gaze softens.

'I have to go,' I say, looking her straight on. 'That's what I do; that's who I am.'

'I suppose so.' She nods weakly, her eyes watering. 'My daughter, solving crimes, one sleepless night at a time... I don't know if I'll ever get used to it.'

Emotions dance in her eyes, concern and worry battling for first place against love and admiration.

I smile as I let go of her hands and step away. 'I love you, Mum. Don't wait up for me.'

'Please be careful,' she says, taking a step forward, her hands reaching towards me on pure reflex.

'Always.' I open the door, turn back to face her with a sly smile. 'Look at it on the bright side, Mum. At least I won't break any ornaments this year.'

———

The Ink Eater is a small bookstore at street level in a one-storey building on Fleet Street, sandwiched between a hairdresser and a kebab vendor. The books in the front window are a bit of a mess, piled haphazardly, and, judging by their covers, not at all recent. Although the sign on the door says 'Closed', Egan asks me to knock.

'Charles is expecting us,' my friend explains.

A little while later, a short man with receding blond hair and a tweed jacket that does little to flatter his plump belly comes to the door. He turns a key in the lock and opens the glass door wide, welcoming us with a warm smile.

'Good evening, Ashford,' he says, reaching for Egan's hand to shake it.

'Evening, Charlie,' my friend replies with a smile of his own. 'Thank you for receiving us so late.'

'But of course.' He waves a hand. 'I'm always open for friends; you know that.' He pauses, and then excitedly adds, 'Especially when it's about trains.'

Egan turns to me. 'This is my partner, Alexandra Neve.'

I smile at the man and extend my hand. 'Pleased to meet you.'

He shakes it energetically. 'Likewise, likewise. It is not often that Ashford brings over friends.'

We exchange a knowing smile at his words before moving further into the store. I watch Charles and Egan and understand that, although college must have been ages ago for them, they have kept in touch. It is evident in the way they greeted each other, and how Charles good-naturedly offered his arm for Egan to take. People who've never dealt with a blind person have the wrong reflexes at first. They try to take the other's arm or hand when it should be the other way around.

The librarian takes us along rows of bookshelves that carve out a maze of corridors through the large open space. The scent of old ink and dust fills the air, bringing with it a feeling of nostalgia. I follow the pair to what seems to be an office. It's a simple room with a desk on one side and a large table in the middle. Shelves filled with what seems to be older, pricier editions cover each wall.

'Your special order hasn't arrived yet,' Charles tells Egan as he stops at the edge of the table. 'But I have received the copy of the latest Dan Brown in Braille you wanted.'

'Ah, good,' Egan says, following along the length of the dark oak with one hand. 'I've been looking forward to this one.'

Egan walks the length of the table until his hand finds the back of one of the two chairs placed around the table. The way he sits down in one fluid motion shows this is not his first visit to this bookstore. Charles motions for me to take the second chair while he perches himself on the corner of his desk.

I smile at the librarian and can't help but say, 'Maybe you could toss in a copy of *Fifty Shades of Grey*, while you're at it?'

Charles chuckles at that, and the mischievous twinkle in his eye tells me he might just follow my suggestion.

'What is it about?' Egan asks, with real curiosity.

'A cosy mystery in a seaside town immersed in fog,' I reply. 'Very interesting; you'll love it.'

Egan shrugs. 'If you think so.'

Out of the corner of my eye, I see that Charles has a hard time containing a giggle as he jots something down on a post-it note. With that, I decide that I like the short man.

'So, you wanted to ask me about the Underground?' the librarian asks, once he's recovered. 'Aren't you full of questions this week?'

'We're working a difficult case,' I edge in. 'You've been of great help so far.'

'Oh, have I?' Charles blushes a little at the praise and readjusts his glasses. 'Happy to help,' he says eagerly, sitting up straighter.

'We're looking for someone who is using the old lines,' Egan says. 'I thought you might have some kind of a map that could help us?'

'From which era?' Charles asks, his voice now serious.

I feel my eyebrow rise in surprise. 'Huh, current, I suppose.'

The librarian frowns and scratches at his temple for a second. He reaches for one of the filing cabinets behind his desk and sifts through some documents before letting out a contented 'Ah!' He turns and faces us, documents in hand.

Moving to the large table, he opens the folder and soon has a large map spread out in front of him. 'This is a current map of the City, with every line of the Underground still in existence.'

I peer at it with curiosity, and recognise Greater London, with the Thames snaking through the middle. Lines are drawn all over the place. The actual Tube lines are easy to recognise: Central, Piccadilly, District. I concentrate on the map and soon discover additional lines and symbols I'm not familiar with; disused stations or portion of tracks I had no idea existed.

'Most Londoners don't know it,' Charles says, 'but there are more than a dozen disused stations under their feet. There are even more disused passageways and shafts.'

'Any lines around Mile End Road and Whitechapel Road?' Egan asks.

Charles points at the map with excitement. 'Oh, yes, there are some old tracks down there. Liverpool Street to Limehouse, and to Pudding Mill Lane, for example.'

'Any disused stations?' I ask.

'Well, let me think.' The blonde man scratches the side of his head again. 'St Mary's was closed in 1938. It was located between Whitechapel and Aldgate East.' He indicates its location with his index finger. 'Oh, and there was Burdett Road, situated between Limehouse and Devons Road.'

'And those platforms and access tunnels still exist?' I demand.

'Oh, yes. Not all of it, but large sections, yes. Some parts have been sealed off with brick walls built at the Tube entrances, but some are simply locked off. The tunnels are kept well preserved for utilitarian purposes. Sometimes they even shoot movies down there.'

The librarian smiles and hits the side of his nose with his index finger, 'And some of the closed entrances aren't so closed anymore. Find the right entry, and you can go down the rabbit hole.'

More seriously, he adds, 'It is not uncommon for squatters and teenagers to break in here and there from time to time. At some point, the police will show up and lock it again, and they'll just start using another entrance. It's like a game of cat-and-mouse.'

'Do you have a more detailed map of the area we're interested in?' I ask, envisioning an oncoming trip below the surface.

Charles sifts through his paper again and hands me, almost reverently, a folded map.

I take it from him and secure it in my inside duffle coat pocket. 'We'll return this to you,' I assure him. 'Thank you so much for your help.'

The librarian nods. 'You're planning a trip to London Below?'

I nod.

His eyes grow round, and he jerks a thumb towards Egan. 'Really?'

I nod again. 'Yes, we are.'

'Take a torch then, and wear some good shoes. I would recommend a safety helmet too. It's a mess down there; not every part is structurally safe.' The way he lists off security measures makes me wonder when *his* last trip down there was. 'Most of the shafts have been tiled off because it was falling down in lumps, but they may have missed some parts. Beware of the lines too; sometimes they turn them back on because they need to divert a train while they're doing maintenance on another line and, trust me, you don't want to step onto those.'

We thank Charles, and leave the small but welcoming store. Egan carries a shopping bag, with a large binder that contains the Braille version of Brown's *Inferno*.

'I suppose there is no way I can convince you to stay at home while I have a look at these disused lines?' I ask Egan, knowing the answer already.

'Nope,' he quips with a resolute smile.

'And you call me stubborn,' I mutter, as we walk down the road with a new purpose.

14

The next morning, we find the maintenance shaft Stenson told us about without too much difficulty. It's sealed by an old emergency door and, as I'd foreseen, the Metropolitan Police have secured it with a heavy chain and a padlock.

'Oh, look,' I say with a forcefully cheerful tone, 'someone put a bolt cutter in my bag, now there's a happy coincidence.'

'You do know this is illegal?' Egan asks, his tone reminding me of my university days.

I cut the chain and hand Egan the bolt cutter. 'Stop complaining, and hold this.' He obliges, and I work the chain free. I have to use both hands to swing the rusty door open. 'Open sesame.'

I place the heavy tool back in the bag and grab a flashlight before leading us both inside. There's a tiny, short concrete tunnel, and then a ladder with iron rungs, which leads downwards.

I get Egan onto it, and follow after him.

'Don't fall on me,' he says as he starts to descend.

'Stop looking at my bum, and get a move on,' I reply, without missing a beat.

The tube we're in seems bottomless; we keep going down and down for what feels like forever. My breath is coming in short puffs when we reach a horizontal tunnel. Down here, the air is cold and damp, with a low oxygen level.

There's no light, and I shine the torch around to get a better idea of our surroundings. Everything is one hundred percent concrete, I note. Charles said it would probably be so, as authorities tend to take London's signature white tiles off for security reasons when they decommission tunnels. Apparently, they can fall off when not maintained, and paperwork would be hell if one were to fall down on a passing City workman.

As we walk further down, there is graffiti on the walls. Some faded, erased by time. Some more recent, perhaps a few weeks old at best.

'We're not the only ones to have been down here recently,' I tell Egan. 'There's graffiti on the walls and discarded junk-food wrappers and beer cans littering the place.'

The tunnel we're in widens as we near what seems to be the entrance to some old platform. It has been sealed off by large brick walls, but the last one is broken.

'Someone's taken a hammer to this wall,' I tell my partner. 'There's an opening big enough to squeeze through.'

'Am I right in supposing you'll want to know what's on the other side?' Egan asks.

'It's kind of fun, don't you think? It's like playing at *Raiders of the Lost Ark*.'

'Hey, I did see that one, as a child,' Egan smiles at me. 'If we happen upon some treasure, please leave it where it is.'

I toss my bag through the opening and help my friend crouch down and get through without injuring himself. I follow him through to the other side.

I flash my torchlight around the empty space and discover I was right; this used to be a platform. An old sign catches my eye, and I squint to make out the words under the dust.

'Welcome to St Mary's Station,' I tell Egan, before flashing my light down the old train tracks. 'Next stop, Whitechapel.'

'If the killer followed this path, and those tracks, he could have gone anywhere once he rejoined an active line.'

It does sound like him. 'Unnoticed and invisible... gone without leaving any trace.'

'Lexa,' Egan reaches for my arm with urgency.

I stop exploring the area and turn back to face him. 'What is it?'

'We're not alone,' he whispers.

I don't see anyone, and can't hear anything, but I trust him anyway. I steer us both to a corner and turn off my torch.

'What can you hear?' I whisper.

'There was a metallic clang,' he says. 'Oh, there it was again.'

'I don't hear anything.'

'It's faint, distant, but growing closer.'

'Train?' I ask, worried.

'No, more like someone hitting a piece of metal against another piece of metal... Ah, there it was again.'

I think I heard it this time, or maybe I imagined it. Either way, if someone's coming, we need a better place to hide —

we're exposed here. I think back on the pitch-black space around us and make an effort to remember the layout.

'Can you tell which way the sound is coming from? Left or right?' I ask Egan, certain this time to have heard a faint clang resound *somewhere* in the distance.

'Left,' he says.

I peer in that direction, but don't see anything. 'If someone's coming, they're bound to have some kind of a light source. They wouldn't be able to see where they're going otherwise. I can't see anything yet.'

There's little time to waste. I turn my torch back on. 'If I can't see theirs, they can't see mine.' I grab Egan's arm and take us to the edge of the platform. 'Come on, jump down.'

With the space around us visible again, I steer us in the direction opposite the noise. 'There's only one way to go; we have to follow the tracks. Keep close to me. We don't know if these are live or not, so we better not touch them.'

I take the lead, and Egan moves to stand behind me. He places his hands on either side of my hips, and I start walking like we're dancing in a conga line. We're forced to move slowly, and I can tell the wooden sleepers are giving Egan a hard time.

'There,' I stop and turn to the left when I spot an opening on the side of the tunnel, 'a maintenance door.'

We sidestep the metallic track and get to the door. It's locked, but the small recess carved into the wall where the door stands should hide us from onlookers. The last thing I see before turning my torch off is the relief on Egan's face at no longer being on the tracks.

Laughter drifts to us in the distance, and a faint glow soon appears in the opposite direction. We're not the only ones walking down the tracks then. Someone else is coming to St Mary's platform from the opposite direction. The occasional word pierces the silence, and the metallic clang now echoes loudly around us.

I can see half of the platform from where I stand. Soon, I make out two teenage boys in the distance. They're under-dressed for the season, wearing warm jackets, but joggers. The shorter one has a baseball cap on his head, twisted sideways. His friend carries what looks to be a beer can in one hand and a long metallic bar in the other. He taps it against the rails every time he feels like it. Well, that answers the question of whether or not the tracks are active.

I suppose they're heading to the brick wall we passed through earlier. I grin as I realise they would have been in for a nasty surprise if some random PI with bolt cutters hadn't opened the door for them.

'Stay here,' I whisper to Egan, before moving back to the train tracks. I take two steps in the darkness to get away from my partner's hideout before flicking my torch back on.

The boys' light is quick to narrow on me. 'Whozthere?' one demands.

'Hi guys,' I reply, as kindly as I can. I show them my empty hands as I keep walking in their direction. 'I'm not a cop, don't worry.'

'Whatcha doing here?' baseball cap asks.

I decide to tell them the truth, hoping curiosity will be enough to keep them from running away. 'I'm a private investigator. I'm looking for a man. We believe he may have used these old tunnels to escape a crime scene.'

'Really?' the kid asks again. 'A PI, like on the telly?'

Not really, no. Sadly, my life is nothing like what Holly-wood makes it look like. 'Yes,' I lie. 'Just like in the movies.'

'Do you have a gun?' the guy with the metal bar asks.

My eyes narrow at him as I pay good attention to his posture and the way he now holds the bar with both hands. I'm being plain, I know, but I want him to realise his move wasn't subtle enough for me. 'Yes, and a taser.' None of it is true, but I square my shoulders and continue with my bluff. 'Trust me; you don't want me to use either on you.'

Both kids look at each other nervously.

'Don't worry, boys; I don't intend to.' I smile at them again, a wide smile. They're teenagers, and I'm a woman; I don't need any weapon, after all. 'I only want to know if you've seen anyone weird down here.'

'B'sides you, ya mean?' baseball cap asks.

I flash him my most charming smile in reply.

'No one,' his friend answers. 'But we don't come here very often. Only when our mum's too busy to take us to Dad's herself. It's a shorter walk down here than up there.'

I had no idea the two teens were related. Now that I'm paying closer attention, I notice similarities in the hard angles of the jawlines and the sharpness of the cheeks.

'Do you know if anyone else uses these tracks?' I ask.

'There are some tramps,' baseball cap says. 'They're staying in the curve, but we never go there.'

'No one else?' I ask.

They shake their heads, and I nod for them to go. They don't wait much longer before scurrying through the hole in the wall.

I turn back to where I've left Egan and see he's already

moved out of his hiding place. He's now standing near the railway track, and I walk back to him.

'Heard everything?' I ask.

'Crystal clear,' he replies.

I give him the torch to hold, while I free Charles's map from my bag. I unfold it and peer down at the disused section we're in.

'There,' I say, pointing down on the map, and feeling very stupid for doing so, seeing as I'm the only one looking at it. 'St Mary's curve; it should be just a little bit ahead.'

I fold the map, and we get moving again. We're advancing a little bit faster now that I know the tracks are safe. Egan stands close to my side, and I steady him when one of his feet catches on a sleeper.

As we move on, I feel something brush against one of my feet, and I just have the time to catch a glimpse of something small and furry with a tail.

I shriek and jump back in terror, my heart beating a staccato rhythm in my chest. The torch jerks out of my fingers and clatters to the ground. It shuts off, shrouding us and whatever else lives down here in total darkness.

'Oh no, oh no, oh no,' I mutter, dropping to my knees.

'What is it?' Egan asks with urgency. 'Lexa, what happened? Are you all right?'

'No, no, no,' I keep muttering, as I start palming the ground around us. The tunnel is pitch-black now, and it seems to darken with every passing second. 'No, no, no, no.'

'Lexa!' Egan asks again, his voice louder this time. 'What is it? What's going on?'

'Rat,' I mutter. *Porca vacca*, could there be more than one? I wonder. Don't think about that, don't think about that.

I keep palming the ground, moving forward on all fours. 'Hate those things.' I keep swiping the ground, my breath picking up, as I try very hard not to think of what else could be lurking about in the dark. Now that I know they're here, I seem to be able to hear them moving, closing in on us... dozens of them, hundreds maybe.

'What are you doing?' Egan asks after I elbow him in the shin in my frantic search.

'Lost the torch — it's gone off.' I move forward, then to one side. When my knuckles violently scrape against the wall, I turn back to where I think the middle is and look there again. 'I can't find it anymore.'

The tips of my fingers hit something metallic, and for a second I feel relief surge inside me, but as I follow down the object's length, I realise it's one of the track's rails. 'Come on,' I urge. 'Where is it?'

For one scary second, I can't remember which side I've already covered. I freeze, turn ninety degrees and resume palming the ground in quick, nervous gestures.

'Lexa, you need to calm down and listen to me.' Egan's voice is loud, and his tone demands my attention.

Desperate, almost out of breath, I force myself to stop my frantic search and listen.

'You're panicking right now and—'

'I'm not,' I interrupt, my words coming out clipped.

'You are,' he says, in a calm voice, reminiscent of his teaching days. 'You need to calm down and act rationally. If you don't use a method to search for the light, you could keep missing it all day.

'Hold still and take a breath,' he continues. 'You were next to me when you lost it, and I haven't moved. That's where you need to look.'

I force myself to slow down and centre myself; then I follow the sound of his voice, scrambling forward on all fours until I reach him.

'Now,' he says, sounding every bit the teacher he used to be. 'Look for the torch intelligently.'

'Left to right?' I start palming the ground around me in a circle. Once the circle is complete, I take a step forward and repeat the motion.

'Left to right,' Egan agrees. 'Calmly and thoroughly.'

It takes two more circuits before the tips of my fingers brush around a familiar object. With relief, I grab the torch and turn it back on.

The tunnel doesn't look so menacing anymore, once bathed in light, and there are no evil rodents ready for a kill in sight. I move back to Egan and squeeze his forearm a second.

'Thanks,' I mutter.

'Welcome to my world,' he says in response.

Feeling a little stupid at my panicked outburst, I clench the lamp hard in my fingers and vow not to let go of it ever again. 'Sorry about that.'

'It's all right.' His hand reaches for my arm, and we start walking again. 'I know darkness can be scary... but rats?'

My skin crawls at the mere mention of the ugly, skittish thing that brushed against me earlier. 'I hate them.'

Egan chuckles heartily at that. 'Could it be the mighty Alexandra Neve is scared of small, innocent rodents?'

'Amnotscared,' I mutter in a rush. 'I just don't like them; they're dirty, and they have beady eyes, pointy teeth, and... and they always look like they're up to no good.'

We keep walking forward, and Egan keeps chuckling.

As we near the impressive curve, light blooms in the distance. Not only light but heat as well. The cold draft that had been constantly blowing, chilling us to the bone, disappears, replaced by faint warmth and the scent of burned wood. The smell of roasted food surprises me soon after.

'The kids told the truth,' I tell Egan, a minute later. 'There are some homeless people gathered here.'

We keep walking and near what can only be described as a camp. 'They've gathered in the middle of the curve. There are mattresses; drapes hung on wires crossing the tunnel from one side to the other; cardboard boxes piled up here and there.'

'A fire too?' Egan asks.

'Yes, in a barrel.' I see it now. 'There are half a dozen people sitting around it. Looks like dinnertime, too.'

We walk towards them in an open manner. There's no need to be discreet as the group noticed us the instant we entered the curve. They give us odd, defiant looks, and seem surprised when they take in Egan's blindness.

A man stands, facing us, while the others remain seated around the barrel. He's the sturdiest of the bunch, and probably the leader of this small community.

'Hello,' I start, keeping my voice quiet and measured. 'My name is Alexandra.'

The man's eyes narrow at me. 'What do you want?'

'This is our place,' one of the men seated by the barrel says. 'You find somewhere else to go; this is our patch.'

The woman seated next to him smacks him on the back of his head, while her free hand clutches an old plaid tightly around her frail shoulders. 'They're not like us, stupid. Look at their clothes.'

She's right; although Egan and I aren't wearing anything ostentatious, our clothes are in better shape than theirs. Our coats are suitable for the season, warm, of adequate length, and they don't have holes in them.

'We mean you no harm.' I turn off my torch, pass it to Egan to hold and lift both of my empty palms to the man facing us. 'We're looking for someone. That's all.'

'Whoever you're looking for isn't here,' the man facing us says sternly.

'Evidently,' Egan can't help but quip. I curse him inwardly as he squeezes my hand.

'We're private investigators,' I confess, taking a few slow steps closer. 'A crime took place on the surface recently. We believe the killer used the tracks to escape.'

'That doesn't concern us,' one of the men sitting near the fire says. He is sitting across from the woman who spoke earlier, and he looks to be in his fifties. His grey hair is a flying mess around his too-thin face.

'None of us committed no crime,' the woman says. From close up, I can see she's missing a few teeth, and the plaid she's wrapped in seems to have had many winters already.

'I know that,' I say, raising my hands in a pacifying gesture. 'I'm not saying you did. We just wanted to know if you've seen something. A stranger, perhaps, wandering the tracks.'

'The only strangers we've seen here are you.' The group's leader crosses his arms over his chest to emphasise how unwelcome we are. 'And we don't like strangers.'

'Please, I promise, we mean you no harm,' I try again. 'We need your help.'

The man scoffs, as the others chuckle. 'Our help.' He laughs bitterly. '*Our* help. Why would we want to help one of *you*?'

'I'm sorry about your situation,' I try, feeling as if I'm hanging by a thread. 'I'm sorry society...'

'You're sorry,' the man interrupts, taking a step closer. 'Sorry doesn't keep us warm at night. Sorry doesn't put food in our bellies. What has sorry ever done for us?' He spits thickly on the floor. 'Well, we are *sorry*, but we can't help you. Now, piss off.'

I take a step back at the man's dark tone and place myself between Egan and him. Damn, the situation could escalate into something nasty. I have a bottle of pepper-spray in my pocket, but that won't be much use against five attackers. Outrunning them is also out of the question given the treacherous terrain. Now, more than ever, I wish I had the gun and the taser I bluffed about earlier.

Egan surprises me by taking a step to the side and coming to stand next to me again.

'Her name was Isabella,' he starts with the same eloquent voice he used to lecture his students. His baritone carries loud and clear through the empty tunnel. 'She was twenty-four when she was murdered. She taught ballet to young girls, and had never done anything wrong in her life. When one of her friends was left without a home after a breakup, she helped him find a new flat and lent him some money.

'Isabella's father died a long time ago, so it was only her and her mother. Now, the poor woman is all alone with nothing but her pain. She doesn't know who killed her little girl, nor why. The police don't have a clue either.

'The only thing we know is what that man, that monster, did to her. How he tortured her, and the two other girls he kidnapped and killed before Isabella. What we know is that it's only a matter of time before he finds another victim.' Egan takes a step forward towards the group, pain, for once, allowed to show openly in the tired lines of his face. 'Please, if you know something that could help us find him, we beg you to tell us.'

The men and women around the fire seem uncertain. Egan's plea has struck a chord. I see two of the women glance towards the youngest man in the group. I move towards him, patting Egan's hand reassuringly on the way.

The brown-haired boy must be about two or three years younger than me. He has tired eyes and hollow cheeks. His clothes are ill-fitting, and the blanket that is wrapped around his bony frame seems too thin for the cold weather.

'What's your name?' I ask him with a warm smile.

'George.' His reply is hesitant, and nervousness ebbs from him.

'I'm not going to hurt you, George.' I smile again. 'Do you know something? Can you help us?'

He shakes his head, almost instinctively.

'If this man uses the tracks to move about the City, you are all in danger,' I tell him and then face the others. 'What is to say the next victim won't be one of you?'

George's nervous gaze shifts to the woman closest to him and then to the man, who is standing too close to Egan for my comfort. After a curt nod from his leader, George looks back to me.

'I saw a man,' he begins. 'Twice. Here on the tracks... only he wasn't one of us.'

'How did you know?' Egan demands.

'We know everyone who sleeps here. We're all regulars,' their leader says.

'That man wore gloves, and a hat,' George continues. 'He had a long coat, in good condition. He isn't one of us.'

'Did you see his face?' I ask. 'Can you describe him?'

'Never, no. The tunnels are dark, and I wasn't close to him. I kept my distance anyway. He had the lapels of his coat high up, and his hat very low. I wouldn't have been able to see much of his face, even if I had been closer.'

'Where did you see him?' I ask. 'Near the old platform?'

'No,' George shakes his head. 'Further ahead, where the line splits in two. The tunnel on the right leads to Whitechapel; the other goes on for half a mile before you hit a brick wall. He was going that way.'

'A dead-end?' I ask. It makes no sense.

'No, just before the wall, there's a small maintenance tunnel. The door's stuck, but if you're thin enough, you can squeeze through. The tunnel behind is tight and in bad shape. Some parts are collapsed, and it's pretty rocky to get out of there, but it leads to the surface.'

'Would we squeeze through?' I ask him.

He gives Egan and me a long look before saying, 'You might just, if you take your coats off.' He jerks his head in the direction of his group's leader and adds, 'Thomas can't get through.'

I look back at the sturdy man, Thomas, and then compare

his body structure to Egan's. My partner is taller, but he is also thinner. It's worth a try.

I turn back to the young man, 'Thank you, George.'

He gives me a shy smile.

I stand back up, reach for my wallet and grab the few notes I have in it. I place them in Thomas's hand, knowing that what I give him will benefit the entire group. I slip him one of our cards too. He doesn't thank me, but gives me a curt nod of acknowledgment.

I give Egan my arm, and we walk back the way we came.

'Be careful, ma'am.' George's voice follows us as we walk away. 'That guy looked shady, and there ain't no good folks who follow the tracks.'

I nod back to him with a smile.

'Fancy a bit of spelunking?' I ask Egan, once we're out of earshot of the group.

'If I say no, will you berate me and tell me how I should have stayed at home?' he demands, with a smile.

'Oh, definitely.'

'Then rest assured that squeezing through tiny spaces and climbing uneven terrain is an absolute dream of mine,' he replies with faked cheer.

We walk back to the platform, continue forward and, within twenty minutes, reach the ajar door George mentioned.

I try to push it open some more, but it doesn't budge. The open space isn't much, and darkness greets us on the other side.

'Are you sure you want to come along?' I ask Egan. 'I could take you back up the way we came, and come back on my own.'

'And risk meeting the man we're after on your own? Nonsense.'

I take off my backpack and squeeze myself through, torch in hand. I manage to squirm through without too much difficulty.

'There's a tunnel all right,' I call back to Egan. I flash my torch about, notice some rubble. It shouldn't be more difficult to navigate this tunnel than the disused tracks we had to follow to get here.

I move back to the other side of the door, grab my backpack and toss it through. Then I move to Egan and reach for the zip on his coat.

He sniggers. 'I'm sure you've always dreamt of doing that, huh, Lexa? Taking my clothes off in some dark abandoned tunnel?'

I recognise the humour for what it is: an attempt at getting our minds off the seriousness of the situation. I play along as I bundle his coat and toss it through the gap. 'Oh, yeah, and on some really wild nights, I even dream that I'm giving you the keys to my mother's car. Now, give me your hands.'

Egan obliges, and I guide him as close to the opening as I can. I place his left hand on the wall, and the other on the opened door, so that he can feel the opening for himself and understand which way he would have to bend to go through.

Under my guidance, he manages, without too much difficulty. I give him back his coat once he's through, and shoulder my bag.

We walk at a slow pace, but steadily progress forward in the tunnel. After some five hundred yards, it starts to tilt upward. There are numerous turns, and the more we walk forward, the more the incline increases.

I wonder how much longer it will take us to get back to the surface, and berate myself for not having asked George that.

I stop dead in my tracks as we round a corner, and the path disappears under a pile of rubble. I shine the torch to the side and notice large cracks in the concrete. Part of the ceiling is collapsed, and we're stuck. A wave of claustrophobia hits me, as I search for a way out.

'Lexa?' Egan asks, 'What is it?'

'Nothing,' I lie, as I force myself to calm down. I still my movements and remind myself to look at the situation rationally. We can always go back. We are not stuck. There is plenty of air to breathe. 'We can't go forward. The tunnel's collapsed.'

'George warned us of that. He said we could go through anyway.' Egan says. 'Isn't there some way to squeeze through?'

I look at the rubble more carefully. 'I don't see anything.'

I take two hesitant steps forward, cautious of where I place my feet. 'Wait.' I move to the far right, bathe the concrete tunnel in light, and finally find it: a narrow gap between a large chunk of the ceiling and the side of the tunnel. '*Porca vacca*, that's tight.'

This is not just some door to squeeze through. The gap is about twenty, thirty feet long. It isn't a straight line either. Some of the iron bars that had been used to strengthen the concrete walls were twisted and broken. They're protruding from the ground, like spikes. In the middle of the gap, an old copper tube that runs from ceiling to floor, probably an old water pipe, has ruptured. Chunks of rusty copper, torn and gaping wide, are just waiting to cut us.

I shouldn't have too much of a hard time to get through, but it'll be a different story for Egan. 'I need you to give me your coat again.'

He obliges, and I stuff it into my backpack. I barely manage to zip the bag closed afterwards. 'All right, I'll go through with our stuff, then come back to get you, okay?'

Egan nods hesitantly. I'm sure he's caught the uncertainty in my voice, and I berate myself for it. I place the torch in his hand, lift his arm up to an adequate height and say, 'Hold it right there.'

I squirm through on my side, half-standing, half-crouching, with the bag in my hand. I avoid the spikes, lean back as close to the concrete rubble as I can to avoid the gaping pipe inches away from my face, then crouch low as I step over some uneven stones. The journey takes me about five minutes, and I'm thankful to be in good physical shape; otherwise, the awkward positions would have me aching all over by now. I toss our stuff to the side, and make the journey back in the same span of time. The torchlight never wavers.

Getting Egan through is a lot more difficult and slow. We take it a step at a time, and carefully execute the movements. Bend your left knee, move your torso to the right, slide towards me. Stop, take one step back, turn your right foot a little clockwise.

I suppose what helps the most is that my partner doesn't see how tight and small the gap around us is. That and the fact he trusts me, and follows my directions to the letter.

We get through eventually, both of us unscathed. The only casualty is his jumper, which got torn by the gaping pipe, a little above the elbow.

The rest of the journey through the tunnel is easier. We keep climbing up, and at some point, I realise we're breathing fresher air. Oxygen-filled air is a nice reprieve from the dusty, wet stuff we have had to make do with since we entered these tunnels. We're soon met by a brick wall and a metallic ladder that climbs up to what looks like a manhole cover.

I give Egan the torch again and climb the iron steps. I struggle to push the cover with my hands. It barely moves. '*Porca vacca*, that thing must weigh a tonne!' I curse, as I turn to try another technique.

'Be careful,' my friend cautions from below.

Precariously, I stand with my back against the ladder. I lower my head and try to push with my shoulders. It sets my back on fire, but it works, and I manage to lift the cover an inch or two, before letting it rest again.

I turn again and look back up. The cover is no longer aligned with the manhole. 'I can see the sky,' I announce, as I reach my fingers through the small opening. I push the cover to the side, and it glides easily. Poking my head out of the hole, I take a deep breath of fresh air and taste freedom.

I climb back down to rejoin Egan and get the torch from him. He climbs up without too much difficulty, and I follow him out.

'Feels good to be out,' Egan says, once seated on a small snowdrift near the manhole. 'Do you know where we are?'

'That's a good question.' I look about, but don't recognise any of the landmarks. 'Some small residential road with houses on both sides. Wait here; I'll go have a look at the crossroad.'

I push the manhole cover back in place, leave my backpack near Egan and follow the road to the next intersection. There, I'm faced with a sign that says 'Mile End Road'. And, just two buildings away, a very familiar church. 'Son of a—'

As I return to Egan, my phone beeps several times. I reach

for it and discover that I have five missed calls and two messages form Stenson. I dial his number.

He picks up on the second ring. 'Alexandra?' he asks, urgency in his voice.

'Yes, what's going on?'

'Where the hell were you? I've been trying to get hold of you all day.'

I look at the manhole cover and try to think of a white lie that wouldn't include breaking into a forbidden old Underground station. 'Sorry, my battery was dead. What's so urgent?'

'There's been another kidnapping.'

15

Stenson joins us an hour or so later at Egan's. He has a grave face; his almond eyes look tired with bags under them that tell me the young man is running on coffee and protein bars, rather than on sleep and home-cooked meals. He carries a folder full of loose sheets of paper under his arm. He starts opening it the minute he sits down.

'You don't have coffee?' he asks as I pour him some tea.

'Haven't you had enough already?'

He looks at me quizzically, and I feel obliged to clarify. 'You look like shit, Matthew.'

He gives me a quick smile and gulps down some of the jasmine tea before returning his attention to the files. 'Another woman has been reported missing. Laurel Stubbs, age 25, from Stratford. Green eyes, blond hair, last seen wearing navy-blue pants and a raspberry jumper.'

'Stratford. He's still shopping in the same area,' Egan says dryly.

'What's her talent?' I ask, certain there has to be one.

'Singer. She was a contestant on one of those talent programs; she made it to the quarter-finals.'

'Oh, I think I remember her,' Egan says.

I turn to face him, surprised. 'You watch reality TV?'

'I listen to it. Laurel Stubbs had a lovely voice, but made poor song choices, despite her coach's advice. With the right songs, she could have gone further in the competition; instead, she stuck to her gospel-ish repertoire all the way through,' my partner continues.

'Either way,' Stenson hands me a missing person's notice with the picture of a young woman that can only come from a professional photo shoot, 'she was popular, and DCS Saunders is pissed off about it.'

I can guess why. 'It'll make it that much harder to keep this out of the media. "Serial killer on the loose kidnaps reality TV star". Yeah, that would look bad.'

'This is most definitely *not* a serial killer case,' Stenson corrects me.

I turn to face him, with a disbelieving look.

'That's the official version,' he adds, looking defeated.

'You're kidding me. People have a right to know what's going on,' I counter.

His look tells me this is an argument he's already had and lost. 'Not according to the powers that be, not two weeks before Christmas.' He passes a bone-weary hand through his dark curls. 'Saunders made that very clear when we had our briefing earlier.'

Egan seems as puzzled as I am. 'You can't be serious.'

'Do you know how many tourists come to London for their

Christmas Holidays? How much Londoners spend in shops during the festive season? Saunders is afraid that if the press catches a whiff of this story, there'll be a media frenzy. It would create a panic that could cost the City millions.

'We have all been instructed to approach this new case as we would any other random kidnapping. At this point, there is no hard proof that Dawn, Carlie and Isabella were killed by the same man. Thus no one should be using the words "serial killer".

'As for Laurel Stubbs, we've been ordered to make sure she didn't run away before we even start talking about a kidnapping.' Stenson sighs. 'Even Langford thinks Saunders is making a mistake this time.'

'All of this so people can spend more money in shops?' Egan says, visibly shocked. 'It's disgusting.'

Stenson passes a weary hand over his face. Tired is not a word strong enough to describe how he looks. 'I told Saunders as much, eloquently so.'

A strange feeling nags at me at his tone. Something rises in the pit of my stomach, and I fear I will not like where this is going.

I do a double take. There is more than fatigue plaguing my friend's face. It's in the set of his jaw, the tight lines around his eyes, and the hollowness in his pupils. He looks like he's just lost faith in what he does; like he no longer believes in the system he serves.

'Saunders must not have been happy with you,' I say.

Stenson laughs dryly. 'Well, I told him what I thought of him, and that conversation almost got me fired. I think I'd have lost my job if Langford hadn't been there to try to calm things down.'

'I'm sorry, Matt.'

'Oh, but you haven't heard the best part yet.' He looks at me with desperate, aching, tired blue eyes. 'I'm off the case.'

'Which one?' Egan asks, with his usual lack of tact. 'Seeing as you have not one but four ongoing cases...'

'All of them,' Stenson bursts out. The fight leaves him just as quickly as it came, and he leans back against the settee, defeated. 'I'm on holiday.'

The words take a minute to sink in. 'You've been suspended?' I ask. 'Now of all times?'

He nods, then gestures to the file he brought with him. 'These are copies I managed to take with me before I left. I had to hide them *underneath my coat*.' The last three words are said with evident disgust. He closes his eyes and massages his temples, exhausted. 'Sometimes I wish I was like you guys; it must be so nice not to have to follow the rules.'

'It must be so nice to have monthly pay and still be able to add to your pension fund,' Egan counters, 'and the resources you guys have are tantalising.'

Stenson doesn't bother reopening his eyes. 'Point taken. So, how did you two spend your day?'

I think back on our little illegal trip through the Underground tunnels and shrug. 'Oh, nothing much.'

'Yeah, right.' Stenson opens one almond-shaped eye to look at me with a raised eyebrow. 'One might find it strange that both of your phones were out of signal all morning.' He lifts a quick index finger. 'Oh no, wait, both of your batteries were dead, right?'

'It happens,' Egan says, with a perfect poker face.

'I'm on holiday, remember?' Stenson closes his eye again. 'I don't arrest people when I'm on holiday.'

'Well then,' I start, 'in that case, we may have taken a trip down some old Tube lines.'

Stenson's eyes flash open at that. 'You what? The Met hasn't gone down there yet, you could have comprom—'

'Holidays, remember,' I cut him short, with a raised palm.

He rolls his eyes then closes them again, and I tell him about our adventure. I tell him how the door our suspect went through could allow him to go to the current Whitechapel Station or, even better, mere feet away from the church where Dawn died. Then I relay, word for word, George's description of a tall man dressed in black. 'At least now we know for sure it was a man,' I finish. 'Although I'd always suspected it was so.'

'What's our next step?' Egan asks, leaning closer.

'The church?' I offer. 'If we continue with our assumption that the killer is a parishioner, we can assume he'll visit that place again. Ground zero and all that.'

Stenson shakes his head. 'I will never manage to convince Langford, let alone Saunders, to authorise a stake-out in front of that building.'

'Well,' I swallow the rest of my tea. 'I guess that only leaves *us* to do the job, doesn't it?'

16

For the next couple of days, Stenson and I take turns watching the House of the Living God, while Egan continues to carry out research. He speaks with Charles again and asks for more information on the old tracks. He contacts DI Carrington to see if she has any nuggets for us — she doesn't. Out of options, he even phones DI Langford to try and get fresh information on how the investigation of Laurel's not–a-kidnapping is going on. Predictably, the inspector isn't very keen to share details, but he does let it slip that the police are at a loss. He also implies that he too believes the four crimes to be connected.

'Nothing new there,' Egan sighed as he reported their conversation.

The last couple of days have been monotonous. I wake up at dawn, drive to the church, and spend most of the day freezing my arse off in my mother's car parked by the kerb.

The first day, I brought a blanket. The next, I brought two

more. No matter how many layers I cover myself in, or how much warm tea I drink, I am still chilled to the bone for hours on end. It is always a relief to see Stenson's dark Volvo park behind me at around two in the afternoon. It announces the end of my shift and the promise of a warm bath to come.

Neither of us catches sight of our mystery man in black. There are very few parishioners. Some regulars show up every day at the same time; others less fervent only come when snowfall and blizzards have been replaced by momentary rays of sun.

As I enter my flat, on the third day of our stake-out, I find my mother busy in the kitchen. She's adding the finishing touches to her famous home-made *pasta carbonara*, and my mouth waters in anticipation. With just one look, I can tell it's the Lexa special, with a little extra cream and salt.

'I love you, mother,' I say, sitting down behind my plate. 'Bath wait,' I add, caveman-like, 'food now.'

My mother chuckles, and a minute later, I have a delicious-smelling plate of pasta in front of me.

'So, you and Matthew are working together again?' she asks between bites. I recognise the lilt of her voice; it's a good indicator that I will not like where this conversation is going.

I try to downplay it as best as I can. 'It's more like I do my half of the stake-out and then he does his. We don't see much of each other.'

My mother continues, unperturbed. 'He's a good man, that one. I like him.'

The way she emphasised "good" makes me want to roll my eyes. Yes, I know my last boyfriend was a degenerate, I feel like saying. I haven't forgotten; there's no need to keep reminding me. I force my mouth to remain shut and hum around a mouthful of pasta.

'Maybe you could invite Matthew over for our Christmas celebrations?' she offers.

I almost spit out the pasta. 'What?'

'Well, Bob is coming, and I hope you have convinced Ashford by now, so what's one more mouth to feed?'

'First Egan, now Stenson? Why don't we just invite the neighbours and put on a buffet?'

'Oh, don't be like that, Lexa.' She flaps a nonchalant hand about. 'It'll be more fun. What could go wrong?'

I ponder the question for an instant. Let's see... Stenson plus me, plus mistletoe in the same room... now throw in Egan and his stupidly obvious innuendos... yeah, what could go wrong, indeed?

I finish my plate without saying another word — which I know my mother will interpret as me caving in and agreeing to her plan — then head for the bathroom. My phone rings as the water is filling the tub. I look between the warm water and the phone. Egan's name shows on the caller ID, and I am almost tempted to let it ring.

'This better be important,' I say in lieu of a greeting. 'You're standing between me and my warm bath.'

'I—I'm hurt, Lexa.' Egan's panting and his tone is far from normal. 'I need you... someone broke in.'

In one swift gesture, I shut the water off and pull the plug. 'I'm on my way.'

I make it to Herbrand Street in record time, even though my friend said at the end of the call that it wasn't too bad — which, coming from Egan, could mean anything from a bumped knee to a bleeding aorta.

I knock at his door and let myself in when there's no answer. I head inside, flicking the lights on as I go. I rush down the corridor, and stop dead when I arrive in the living room. What I catch sight of then has me gasping in panic.

The place is a mess. There's no other word for it. Everything has been thrown about and — my breath catches in my throat — there are drops of blood going from the open window to the corridor that leads to the bedroom and bathroom.

'Ash?' I ask, my voice borderline panicky. 'Ash, where are you?'

There's no answer, and I quickly look at the kitchen on my right. Empty. I move forward then, follow the corridor. I find the bathroom door half open and blood on the door handle.

I push it open and rush in to find Egan passed out near the toilet. A first-aid kit has been tossed open on the rug, and some gauze is wrapped around his right hand in a jumble.

'Ash!' I cry out, kneeling next to him.

There's no reply and my fingers desperately reach for the side of his neck. I find a strong, quick pulse beating underneath the thick turtleneck pullover.

I sigh in relief, and shake his shoulder to try and rouse him. I get a moan out of him and with a little more prodding, his eyes blink open.

'Ash, it's me, Lexa. Are you all right?'

I get a confused, stuttered jumble of incoherent words in reply.

'What the hell happened?' I ask, helping him sit straighter.

I reach for his hand and unfold the gauze. The skin underneath is bloody, and I find a large cut on his palm. It's bleeding, and I tighten the gauze back in place.

'Cut my hand,' Egan mumbles. 'Hurts.'

'I think it needs stitches,' I tell him.

'No. It's just... I have thin blood. It'll take a bit to coagulate.' Egan explains, and his voice sounds thick. 'I don't handle blood loss very well.'

He waves his free hand up and down, encompassing himself, and I take it as an explanation for his passing out before I arrived.

'What happened here?' I ask while I sort through my friend's first-aid kit for something I could use.

'I don't know,' he replies with a smile that says I'm stupid for asking. 'What does it *look* like?'

'Like some rock star decided to trash his hotel room for the fun of it?' I drop my bag and coat in the empty bathtub, and kneel back down. 'How'd you cut your hand?'

'On some glass, although, I'm not sure where it came from,' he replies. 'Can you get me a glass of water? It'll help get my pressure back up.'

I trot back to his kitchen and instead manage to find a Coke in one of the cupboards. He frowns upon the first sip.

'Sugar will help,' I assure him.

Colour returns to his cheeks, and I look at his hand again. He was right; blood has finally started to coagulate on the sides of the two-inch cut.

It looks as if Egan palmed broken glass. I clean the cuts, find two small pieces of glass embedded in his skin, and remove them with tweezers. I clean the cuts again and bandage his hand securely.

Egan is a perfect patient. He doesn't say a word, and only hisses once or twice. He seems content to let me focus on the task at hand while he sips his Coke.

As I clean his palm, I can't help but notice tiny little scar lines here and there. They have faded with time, but are still visible. They bring back the story he told me of his time in China, and make me wonder if he got them as he crawled out from under the rubble.

'There you go,' I say, letting go of his hand, after one last satisfied look. 'All patched up.'

He flicks a feeble smile my way, though he remains nervously tight. 'Thank you.'

'Now, do you mind telling me what the hell happened here?'

'Wish I knew.' He shrugs his shoulders. 'I went to Charles's to return the map and ask him a few more questions. When I came back home, nothing was in its place anymore. There was a draft, so I went to close the window. I think it must be broken, because I cut myself.'

I hadn't noticed the broken window, but then there was so much to take in. I close the first-aid kit, place it back where it belongs, then offer Egan my arm and walk him back to the main room.

'The window?' Egan asks.

I turn to my right and note that one of the two large windows on either side of the TV is broken. There are shards of glass on the floor and on the windowsill. I catch sight of my friend's blood on the latter.

'One's broken. It's a good thing you had shoes on.'

'And the rest of the place?'

'Well...' I glance about. 'Do you remember that time my flat was ransacked, when we were on the Ruby Heart case?'

Egan hums.

My place had looked like a hurricane had dropped by for a visit. 'Well, your living room pretty much looks the same.'

I take two more steps forward until I reach Egan's upturned chair. I reach down for it and return it more or less to its rightful place. After I place my friend's hand on its back, he sits down with a defeated look.

'Tea?' I ask.

'If whoever did this didn't steal the kettle, yes please.'

I move to the kitchen — then stop dead in my tracks.

'At least there's no death threat written in blood-red paint this time,' Egan mutters to my back, referencing the message that had been left on the door of my flat.

It breaks my heart to have to disagree. 'No. They didn't choose red this time.'

I had missed it when I first entered the room, as I wasn't looking in the right direction. Now I see it, plain as day. A dagger has been planted in my friend's library; it holds a note in place.

I take a step forward to make out the words written in black ink. "Stop looking for us. J."

I read the note out loud and reach for my phone, only to realise I left it in my coat pocket, which is still next to the bath-tub. I turn round and search for Egan's. I find it in its usual place. Somehow the three little purple bowls atop the low wall that separate the kitchen from the living room survived the trashing. I dial Stenson's number and curse when the call goes to voicemail. I leave him a terse recap of what happened.

I turn back to face Egan. 'All right, pack a bag; you're coming to stay with me.'

'Lexa, I—'

'Don't!' I cut him off. 'Someone broke into your flat, and we both know who that someone is. He knows we're onto him.'

Another frightful thought assaults me. 'If he knows where to find you, that means he knows where to find *me*. My mother is alone at home right now, and I won't let anything happen to her.'

I find that the coat hanger has been tossed to the other side of the room; Egan's thick winter coat made half the distance, landing in a lump near the upturned coffee table. I reach for it and drop it on my friend's lap.

'I'm not going to leave my mother alone and unprotected, and I'm not going to leave you here alone either. Do you see where I am going with this?'

Egan stands with a grumble and shrugs the coat on. We're off ten minutes later.

It's half-past eight when we make it to Camden Street. I'm relieved to find my mother dosing off, watching some stupid dance show on the telly when I enter the flat.

'Not a word,' I whisper to Egan, as I notice her rousing.

My mother blusters when she finds I'm not alone. She tries to rearrange herself, patting down her greying hair and tiding up her clothes, like that matters with Egan. I can't help but shake my head and smile fondly at her.

'Good evening, Ashford,' she says, recovering. 'Isn't it a bit late for a house call?'

'Evening, Laura,' he replies.

My mother catches sight of his suitcase before he has time

to elaborate. Next, she sees the bandage on his hand, and a frown appears on her brow. 'Did something happen?'

Egan lifts his hand up, unaware that my mother had already caught sight of it. 'Hurt myself when I broke a vase. A very stupid accident, but it's going to make things difficult for me. Your daughter kindly offered to play nurse.'

I grab Egan's suitcase and take it with me to my room. 'I'll get the folding bed out and pop it in my room.'

As I set to work, I hear my mother and Egan make small talk in the living room. I'm finishing buttoning the pillowcase when my partner enters the room.

He closes the door behind him, and stands poised there. 'I'm not entirely sure she believed me,' he whispers.

'Well, you know what they say; the apple doesn't fall far from the tree,' I chuckle, knowing how hard it is to get one past her. 'Three steps forward, two to the left,' I tell him. 'She'd better believe it; I don't want her to worry for nothing.'

Egan follows the direction and soon finds the bed. He sits down next to me. 'It would hardly be "for nothing".'

'We're both here, and I'll sleep with my eyes open. We're safe for the night. I'll get Matthew's opinion tomorrow, and find some way to get my mother out of harm's way.'

'Still no answer from him?' Egan asks.

I tried to reach Stenson two more times since we got back to the flat. 'No, I keep getting his voicemail.'

'That worries you.'

My nerves crack a little at the question. 'He's on a stake-out in front of a church where nothing interesting ever happens, so yes, it worries me that he's not picking up.'

'Keep your voice down,' Egan cautions, jerking a thumb in the general direction of the door.

I take a deep breath to calm myself. 'Do you think something could have happened to him? If the killer found us, he could know Matthew's watching the church.'

Egan takes his time to answer. He leans forward, rests his elbows on his knees, and cradles his hurt hand in the palm of the other one. 'What I don't understand is how.'

'How what?'

'How did the killer know we were after him? None of this is in the press. Hell, even the police are doing a bodged job of finding him...'

I try to follow his chain of thought. 'We are the only ones trying to do it right, but how would he have known that? Do you think he saw us investigating?'

'And what?' Egan asks. 'He singled us out amidst all the policemen and detectives then found out my address?' He shakes his head. 'No, something's not right. Besides, it's usually your place that gets it, not mine.'

I can't help but chuckle at that. My partner's right, though. It's my address embossed on the business cards we keep handing out to people. It is my flat that has been ransacked during previous cases. 'I see your point.'

As I try to think it through, I move to my own bed, kick off my shoes and lie down on my back. 'We've been asking a lot of questions and handing out our cards left and right... Could the killer be one of the people we met? Or maybe he's close to one of the persons we interrogated?' The ceiling I'm staring at provides no answer.

I hear the folding bed creak, and surmise Egan must be

trying to get comfortable as well. 'Again, why my flat and not yours?'

'You're right; that doesn't make sense. Why go to the trouble of finding your address when mine would have worked just as well?'

'What was the message again?'

'"Stop trying to find us,"' I repeat. 'It was signed "J."'

'Who would be stupid enough to sign that note?' my friend asks.

He's got a point. Although it was only an initial, it was stupid to sign the note. 'Someone *not* in his right mind. And if there's one thing we're sure of, it's that the killer we're after isn't sane.'

'But he's made no mistakes so far,' Egan counters. 'Remember what the police said: no evidence.'

'Because the murders were carefully planned. Breaking into your flat was rash, unprepared.' I think back on how the living room had looked; things had been tossed aside for the sheer sake of it. 'It was an impulsive decision. I think we pissed him off.'

'So now what — we have an unhinged psychopathic killer after us?'

I snort derisively. 'Makes for a more interesting day.'

My friend remains silent awhile, as we both get lost in our own thoughts. Is there really a chance we put ourselves in the killer's line of sight? We do not fit his victim profile; could that be enough to get us safely through this case? Or could he want to take us off the investigation in a more drastic way regardless of our lack of talent?

'Something else puzzles me,' Egan says. 'His use of the plural form.'

'Yeah, that bothers me too.'

'We never considered there could be more than one killer... I'm not particularly fond of that new theory.'

'I don't see how that would work.' The planning, the careful selection of victims, the staging. 'This killer fulfils very specific needs by committing those monstrosities. How could two people have that very same need? It makes no sense. Besides, George only ever saw one man.'

'Maybe J has an ally; someone covering up for him?' The bed creaks again. 'Maybe that's what "us" means.'

I wriggle my phone out of my back pocket. 'I wish Matthew would pick up his damn phone already.' I try the number again. 'He could have an idea.'

'Voicemail?' Egan asks as he hears me curse in very colourful Italian.

I don't say anything, and toss the cell phone aside. The silence stretches as we both contemplate the darkness we're in and try to make sense of this leadless case.

How could a man who is stupid enough to sign his death threats be, at the same time, a perfect killer who leaves his murder scenes squeaky clean? It doesn't add up. And the police, let's face it, are being overzealous in their incompetence. Missing reports, investigations misled — that too has me confused.

'Once you've ruled out the impossible...' I mutter to the darkness.

'So, are you going to voice aloud the thing we're both pretending we haven't thought of?' Egan asks me.

I blow out a loud breath, wishing his words and what they imply away.

'I thought about it, and I know you must have as well,' Egan continues. 'It could be *him*.'

Him — London's most wanted man — the puppet master who pulls all the strings from somewhere in the darkness. The Sorter.

'We have no way of being certain he's involved,' I say.

'And yet...' Egan lets his words hang heavy in the air.

I thought about it too, of course. It would make sense, in a sick, twisted way. He's contacted us before – and even though his love notes have always been sent to my home, it isn't much of a stretch to assume he knows where Egan lives; he's thorough like that.

When my best friend, Irina Anderson, was murdered, the Sorter had been the one connecting the British bankers and Russian arms dealers that were behind it. When a former Nazi soldier wanted to get his hand on a special necklace last summer, it had been the Sorter who put him in touch with the right thief for the job. He is London's number one criminal matchmaker, but that's not all. His involvement runs a lot deeper than that. In both cases, he also provided customer support along the way and monitored the police investigations to make sure there would be no witnesses. Hell, there might even be a free phone number you can call if you've messed up your mischief.

"Don't worry about the Met. The Boss has them covered," I heard one of the Russian thugs say during Irina's case.

'We've always assumed the Sorter has inside information,' I say. 'A person or more within the police on his payroll. In this instance, it could explain the missing reports.'

'It's the little details...' Egan's voice is faint, giving me the impression he's thinking out loud. 'It's always the little details that betray us — tiny things that get overlooked in favour of the bigger picture.

'There is no proof the Sorter exists, yet everyone knows he's there. He's like a black hole. You can't see it, but you can prove its existence by the impact it has on its surroundings... it's the details you can't hide.'

'Something doesn't fit the pattern, though,' I say. 'What does he have to gain in participating in this killing spree?'

This is the one thing that doesn't add up. There can be no end game, no big scheme, and, more importantly, no profit. 'The killings are done to fulfil some sick needs; victims meet specific criteria. At no point should our killer have need of outside help... yet the note said *us*.'

Egan hums in thought. 'Do you think he hired the Sorter as a possible get-out-of-jail-free card? That his task is to make sure the police won't close in on him?'

I ponder the thought and try to imagine what the killer could look like, what his lifestyle could be. I picture him as a recluse, a loner... a shady character who likes to dress up in black and crawl through Underground tunnels to remain unseen.

Once more, it doesn't add up. 'Do you think our killer would have enough money to hire the Sorter?'

'That seems unlikely,' Egan agrees. 'Yet, I don't see the Sorter working for free.'

'Repaying a favour?' I think it through then dismiss the idea. 'No, the Sorter isn't the type of man to have debts.' I punch my pillow. 'Damn it. We're clutching at straws here. Could they know each other? Could they be friends somehow, or...'

I'm interrupted by the sound of my phone ringing. I'm surprised not to recognise the number as I'd been hoping for Stenson's.

I hit the answer button. 'Alexandra Neve.'

'It's Langford. Get your arse to the church, pronto! Something's happened to Stenson,' the DI grumbles, and then he shuts the communication.

17

Although it's past midnight, and the streets are deserted, the journey takes longer than I would like. I wish I could drive at rocket speed, but a) my mother's old Fiat Punto is not a rocket, and b) it's started snowing again. I'm forced to muddle through at a prudent, within-the-speed-limit pace. Too bad Egan didn't come along; he'd have been pleased at my sensible driving, but caution had me leave him with my mother, just in case.

As I round the corner, I see an ambulance departing. My heart clenches when I realise it doesn't have the sirens on and drives away at a speed that matches mine. It tells me there's no one fighting for his life inside. Were they too late, then? Has Stenson...? Is he...?

No! He has to be all right. How else would Langford have found my phone number? Stenson must have given it to him, right? Yes.

That comforting thought only lasts until I remember

Stenson likes to carry some of my business cards with him. He hands them out to people he can't help but who could benefit from our way of investigating.

Could Stenson be... I can't form the thought, even in my own head. I park the old Punto behind a yellow and blue police car, slam on the breaks and exit in a rush.

Stenson's dark Volvo is there, a little ahead. There's another car parked next to it. I think I recall seeing it before, and surmise it must be Langford's. I push forward, find a gathering of policemen near the church's entrance and walk up to them.

Relief surges through me when my eyes settle on one very much alive Detective Sergeant Matthew Stenson. He's sitting on the entrance steps to the old building and holding what looks like an icepack over a bandage on the side of his head.

'Matthew,' I mutter breathlessly, 'what happened?'

Four pairs of eyes turn my way, but I only care for one. I dismiss the two constables standing nearby and the inspector leaning heavily on the stair railing.

'Got knocked out,' Stenson says, moving the ice pack away from the bandage for emphasis. 'I'm seeing stars at the moment, but I'll be fine.'

I stop near the first step, feeling awkward and suddenly unsure of myself. I turn a murderous gaze towards DI Langford, but he ignores me. The smug bastard could have told me that Stenson was okay over the phone. Why the hell did he have to be so evasive? I wonder if he gets off on antagonising me.

The adrenaline rush is receding, and I'm now taking full notice of the curious looks directed my way. I look down, shifting from foot to foot.

'You're just seeing Christmas lights,' Langford mutters,

turning his attention to his DS. 'Medic said it's just a bump, so stop being a wuss about it.'

He turns to the two nearby constables and starts to bark orders at them. 'I want the full zone secured, and a team of forensics here within the hour!'

They give him a curt, 'Yes, sir,' and get to work with practised efficiency.

'Now,' he turns back to face his subordinate, 'start back from the beginning.'

'I got lucky on my watch,' Stenson starts. 'Around ten twenty, I noticed a figure — a man in a black trench coat, hat low on his head — walking down the street. He was keeping to the shadows, trying to hide his face. I watched him walk up the steps of the church and go inside. It was locked for the day, so he must have used a key to get in.'

I take notes.

Stenson moves the icepack away from his head and lets it drop to his feet before continuing. 'I waited for a beat and followed him inside. I saw no one. I found the entrance to the stairway at the back of the church. There seemed to be a flicker of light down there, so I went down.' He licks his lips, and I can guess his head injury is giving him a hard time because he blinks a lot too. 'I arrived in some dark room, with lit candles on each side. I entered, as silently as I could. The room was empty, save for a chair and a table with an open bible on it. I was looking at it when a man came in from behind me.' Stenson shudders. 'I only had a second to see his face before he knocked me out.'

'Do you remember it?' Langford asks. 'What he looked like?'

'I'll never forget it.' Stenson looks up, staring at us with an intense gaze. 'I've never seen anything like it. His face was so horribly scarred; covered in burns, his whole face... the flesh thick and disfigured. When I came back around, the man was gone, the church's doors left hanging open.'

'Burned?' Langford echoes.

Stenson's face turns sickly. 'Yeah, like nothing I've seen before. No more hair — just scarred skin that made him look barely human.'

'If his entire body was badly burned, it would explain why he never left any prints on the crime scenes; why you couldn't even find a hair,' I say, offering Stenson what I hope is a comforting smile.

He reaches down for the icepack again.

'Well, that changes things.' Langford reaches into his coat pocket for his phone. 'If he was the victim of a fire, he'll be on record somewhere.' He takes a few steps away and starts barking orders into his mobile for whoever's on the other end of the line to search for a male fire-victim who would present severe burns all over his body, between the ages of twenty to fifty.

I take the opportunity to move closer to Stenson. 'Are you okay?' I ask. 'I was worried when Langford called.'

'Yeah, sorry about that.' He shrugs. 'I had to call it in, holiday or not. He forbade me from warning you before he got here.'

'Bastard!' I blurt out, loud enough for the nearby DI to overhear.

Stenson seems surprised at my outburst.

'He made it sound like you were dying or something,' I explain. 'How's the head?'

'I see stars.' He flashes me a smile that's meant to be reassuring. 'And you're the prettiest of them all.'

'And you're clearly concussed,' I reply, feeling my cheeks flame.

Stenson's smile dies quickly. The corners of his almond eyes are pulled tight, a definite indicator of the pain he's in.

'What did Langford want me here for anyway?' I ask.

'I had to tell him you carried out half of the stake-out. He said he wanted to know if you've seen anything interesting.'

'Nope,' I snort. 'I got the boring half, and you got the exciting one.'

Stenson's chuckle is short-lived. 'Talking about halves... where's your better one?'

'Long story...' Out of the corner of my eye, I see Langford coming back, and cut it short. 'Now's not the time.'

Stenson nods in understanding.

'We should have a list of names within the hour,' the DI says.

'That's a good start.' I nod.

Langford rounds on me in quick fashion. 'Oh, no. I don't care what your involvement has been so far: it ends now!'

'Inspector,' I try.

'No. You two PIs in training have done enough. I want you out of my sight and away from my men!'

I cross my arms over my chest and thank the stars I'm a good head taller than the plump DI. I stare him down, hard. 'No.'

His round eyes narrow under his rimmed glasses. 'What did you say, *kid*?'

My jaw tightens at the stupid nickname, and my voice rises in volume. 'I said no. We've been working our arses off on this case — you don't get to bench us now. We were right about the church, we were...'

Langford grabs me by the arm before I have the time to utter another word. He yanks me forward and leads me away from the church and Stenson, who looks too dazed to protest.

Langford may be shorter than me, but he has more strength, and there isn't much I can do to stand my ground. He's furious, red-cheeked —I find myself expecting to see foam forming at the corners of his mouth.

'Get your hands off me.' I try to push him away.

He doesn't let go, takes a step forward, his eyes boring into mine. 'You've done enough!'

'Let go of me,' I repeat, contemplating using one of the Wushu moves I've learned where you kick your opponent in the knee to make him lose his balance.

'You will stand down *now*,' he continues, as if I hadn't interrupted, 'and leave my sergeant out of your schemes.'

'Matthew was just doing his job.' I'm drawn into the conversation. 'Investigating these murders is what *you* should have been doing.'

The DI lets go of my arm and raises his hands up in a wide arc. 'Oh, you think you're so much better than the rest of us, don't you? You've solved one or two cases, so you're as good as trained policemen, right?'

'Twenty-four,' I say, just to spite him, crossing my arms again.

'What?'

'Twenty-four solved cases in less than ten months. What's your record like, inspector?'

'Who bloody cares?' Langford roars. 'We're not keeping scores; we're doing our jobs.'

He barely has the time to finish his sentence before I fire,

'Your job is to find a serial killer, not to play Saunders' twisted political games and pretend all is well in our merry City.'

'I don't need you to tell me how to do my job. I've known all along these cases were connected. Or did you think I was born yesterday?' He balls up his fists at the end of his tirade, and I wonder whether a punch is imminent.

Would pepper-spraying an infuriating detective inspector be a crime worthy of jail time? Probably not, right?

'You and your cute blue eyes,' Langford continues, fists balled up, 'you just had to bat your eyelashes at him, didn't you?'

'What?' I ask, feeling my cheeks tinge red.

'I should have known Stenson wouldn't stay at home like he promised. I should have known he'd try to help you.'

I let the first sentence pass me by and focused on the second half of his rant. 'A bloody good thing he did. He got us our first breakthrough in this case.'

'You're a bloody danger magnet, *kid*,' Langford spats.

The sentence freezes me. The words are echoes of an earlier conversation. Langford's called me a danger magnet once before, months ago, while we were on another case. He'd been right to — less than an hour later I got myself kidnapped and nearly died.

Despite myself, I swallow some of my pride and look away.

'I don't care if you were right, if this was the right place. One of my men got hurt tonight,' the inspector continues. 'The police have procedures and rules to be followed to avoid this kind of mess. We don't do stake-outs *on our own*; we don't follow suspects *alone*.' His voice rises in volume to make sure I get the point. 'And we never enter possible danger zones without a partner at our back!'

He has to take in a breath after that one.

'My sergeant could have died tonight,' he starts barking at me again. 'What good would you have been then? Would you have brought him back to life? Would you have been the one to go and break the news to his folks?'

The fight dies in me at the inspector's harsh but true words. I hadn't considered that angle, and feel lousy for realising too late in how much danger I put my friend.

I manage to choke out a derisory, 'M' sorry.'

'Yeah, well sorry ain't going to cut it when someone turns up dead. You're out!' With those last parting words, Langford turns his back on me and storms over to one of the officers hovering near the patrol car.

I'm too dumbstruck to say anything. I swallow down the man's words, and feel like shit. First Egan gets hurt, and now this. In frustration, I kick furiously at a nearby snowdrift. All I manage to accomplish is to hurt my foot.

It is with a slight limp that I walk back to Stenson, who's still sitting on the stairs. He sports a forlorn expression and, for the second time tonight, I wonder if maybe he should get checked for a possible concussion.

'Did the paramedics clear you?' I ask.

'Yes. There's a short list of things I need to be on the lookout for, and I'm not supposed to sleep for a little while... want to keep me company?' He tries to smile again, but it falls short once more. 'Don't worry — it's not a first.'

He stands up, looking away at one of the policemen who is taking pictures of the church's door. The icepack remains forgotten on the concrete steps.

'Don't mind him, Alex,' Stenson says, stepping down the

stairs. 'He's all bark but no bite.'

I keep staring down at the icepack; my mind is stuck on different scenarios with worse endings.

'Don't let it get to you.' The young man nudges my arm. 'I heard most of what he said — it isn't like that at all. I knew what I was getting myself into; I knew the risks, and I accepted them.'

I raise my eyes, ready to reply in kind, ready to beg Stenson to hate me, to get as far away from the danger magnet as he can.

He silences any protests I could have uttered with a murmured, 'And I would have done it, even if your eyes were green,' and he kisses me.

The world stops turning for a few seconds. I close my eyes, lean forward, and for a short moment, which feels like a small eternity, everything is perfect in my world. Killers and criminal masterminds are forgotten, and all I can think of is Matthew Stenson. He takes all of my mental space; I see his face, smiling at me, the dimples at the corners of his lips. His hands on my shoulders radiate warmth, and his lips feel like... well, there isn't a word strong enough, beautiful enough to describe that feeling.

The moment soon ends and our lips part. I'm left with an aftertaste of mint on my tongue and weak knees.

'You're an idiot,' I manage, once I've recovered enough to take in a deep breath. I feel my cheeks burn and hope the dim light surrounding us will be enough to hide it. As first kisses go, that wasn't bad.

Stenson chuckles as we walk back to my car. 'An idiot I may be, but I'm not a child. I'm a trained detective, and I have a job to do.'

'You're on holiday, remember?' I tease him.

He huffs, rolls his shoulders and checks that the bandage is still secured. 'I think I'm done with that. I'm the only one who can ID our suspect; Langford wants me back in the field, and holidays are boring anyway.'

I reach for his arm to halt him. 'Matthew, your injury.'

'It's just a bump — nothing severe. I'll have a headache for a day or two, but I've had worse. You should go home while I wrap things up here. It's best if you stay out of Langford's hair for a while.

'I'll drop by your place tomorrow and give you the latest news, okay?' he adds, his tone serious now. 'We need to wrap things up in the church.'

I nod, go to get in my car, then stop as a thought hits me. *The church...* I turn back to face Stenson. 'There was a nun.'

His eyebrows shoot up, and he grimaces a second later as the movement jars at his injury. 'What?'

'In the church, the first time Ash and I came here. We asked her questions, but she said she didn't know much. She seemed okay to me, but I remember Ash felt something odd about her.' I push my hands in my pockets. 'I didn't think it was important; had forgotten about it until now... maybe you could try to find out more about her? Just in case.'

He nods gravely. 'I will. Do you remember her name?'

'Sister Anne.' I offer him one last smile, as a goodbye, and start to get into my car.

'It was a good idea to watch the church, Alexandra,' Stenson calls back after me. Although I'm two feet away from him, his voice is loud enough for everyone in the vicinity to hear. 'You were right — thanks.'

'Stenson. Report. *Now!*' Langford barks, even louder, from somewhere to my left.

18

S tenson stops by my flat the next morning, and I show him the note we found at Egan's. I had wrapped it in a plastic evidence bag to keep any possible fingerprints or DNA traces intact.

He frowns as he silently reads the words. 'You should have called me right away.'

I roll my eyes. 'I tried — only you were too busy getting yourself knocked out by our killer.'

Stenson stares at me with a blank look. Next to him, Egan sighs loudly.

I give the sergeant an apologetic smile. 'Okay, not funny, sorry. Did you guys find anything at the church?'

Stenson shakes his head. 'No, but we're still looking. The place is under lockdown and is being processed by Forensics.' He looks down at the note again. 'I should call in a team to your flat, Ashford. Look for prints or anything else that could help.'

My partner tenses at the words. I can imagine how the idea of even more strangers disturbing his sanctum must feel to him.

'I'd rather you didn't,' he says, hoping against hope.

'He may have made a mistake this time,' Stenson tries. 'There could be something.'

'We all know there won't be,' Egan retorts, more strength to his voice now. 'Please — it's been ransacked enough as it is.'

I search for Stenson's eyes and motion for him to let it go. 'He's right; there won't be anything. Our man's too clever for that. We all know it.'

Although he clearly isn't pleased, Stenson lets us have it our way. 'Fine, but I'll have the note analysed, just in case. I have a friend in the Forensics department who owes me one; he'll keep it off-the-record.'

I offer him a silent 'thank you,' in reply.

'What bothers us the most,' Egan says, evidently relieved, 'is that he went to my place instead of the *Casa Neve*.'

'You're not in the Yellow Pages, are you?' Stenson asks.

Egan shakes his head. 'I've been off it for years; since I started teaching at the university actually.'

'That doesn't make it impossible to find you,' the sergeant says, 'just a little more difficult.'

I lean forward but keep my eyes downcast. 'It wouldn't be hard for someone who works for the Metropolitan Police, would it?'

Stenson pauses for a moment, his brow furrowing. 'What are you implying, Alex?'

'You know very well what I'm implying,' I reply. 'You were in that warehouse with me last winter; you heard it too.' His glare darkens, and I continue, quoting word for word what the

Russian arms dealer said that day: '"Don't worry about the Met. The Boss has them covered."'

'It could have meant any number of things,' Stenson says.

I don't understand why he seems so cross. Egan and I have been entertaining for months the idea that the Sorter has one or more informants, and it's not the first time our sergeant friend has heard it. 'You know very well what it meant — we all do.'

He huffs, closes his eyes and gives me a pinched smile. 'Fine.' His eyes open again and narrow on me, 'Then, pray tell, what is the Sorter's interest in this?'

I curse inwardly. Of course he had to press his finger on the one thing we hadn't been able to figure out yet.

'We aren't sure,' Egan replies in a level voice. 'Now, if I may add to this fruitful conversation,' he continues, taking on a lecturing tone, 'and continue with the assumption that the Sorter is involved, and factor in what we know of his modus operandi, couldn't there be a thing or two to be said about the way this investigation has been handled by the Metropolitan Police? It seems to me that this serial killer was either born under some very lucky star, or someone has been pulling strings for him all along and making sure his crimes would be investigated as slowly as possible...'

I catch on to my partner's train of thought and finish his sentence for him, 'By not considering the serial killer angle, and treating each disappearance separately, starting anew each time.'

'*Divide and conquer* is a motto that has been proven efficient time and time again,' Egan agrees. 'History is full of very good examples.'

I look up to Stenson, who remains silent. His face looks troubled; it's as if he's weighing up each argument.

'That's a little farfetched, don't you think?' he says. 'You have nothing solid.'

I open my mouth to retort, but Egan beats me to it.

'There's more, isn't there?' Egan's eyebrows disappear behind his dark glasses, the sign of a frown that can only mean one thing: he's heard something in Stenson's voice that doesn't add up. 'What are you not telling us, Sergeant?'

I turn back to face Stenson, narrowing my eyes and challenging him to pretend he's not keeping something from us.

'Fine, fine.' Stenson lets out a long breath. 'You remember that order Langford gave last night?'

'Which one?' I demand. 'His rant was quite long.'

'Not to you — when he called back to New Scotland Yard?'

Last night was very eventful, and I have to think a little before answering. 'He wanted someone to look at the records, find men who were badly burned. Have you found our suspect?'

Stenson shakes his head. 'No. Results came in this morning; no man matching my description was found within Greater London.'

'He may have been born outside of the City,' Egan says.

Stenson nods. 'That's why we extended the search. We found a few matches, but they all live way out of town. We found nothing.'

That triggers a not-so-distant memory. 'Just like you didn't find the connection between Dawn and Carlie — another error in your database, maybe?'

'Seems like a lot of those are happening lately,' Egan quips.

Stenson rubs a weary hand over his face. 'Either way, even if any of this is true, we have no way of identifying the mole.'

'But we know where the orders came from.' I point out.

Almond-shaped blue eyes narrow on me fast, surprise clouding the pupils. 'Please tell me, I beg of you, that you are *not* suggesting that Detective Chief Superintendent Saunders — a man who's had a desk at Scotland Yard for the past twenty years or so, who boasts an exemplary career — could be involved in any of this?'

I shrug. 'Maybe not him; maybe someone who works for him, someone he listens to...'

'No,' Stenson cuts in. 'I refuse to believe this. Saunders may not be seeing things very clearly, because of the tight spot he's in, but he's no mobster's patsy. Not him.'

The outburst surprises me, and I choose to offer no reply, allowing the argument to come to an end, for now.

'We're wasting our time talking about this. We should be focusing on this.' Stenson waves the note he's holding for emphasis. 'I'll get it to our lab and see if they can find prints on it, or anything else useful.'

'Doubt it,' I edge in.

'In the meantime,' he continues, as if I hadn't interrupted, 'you guys need to be on your guard. These types of warnings are not to be taken lightly.'

'Alexandra has offered to put me up for a few days,' Egan says.

'And I sold my mother on the idea of spending a few days with her boyfriend until Christmas to share the festive cheer and all that.'

'Good,' Stenson nods before standing up. 'You two need to stay together, and be on the lookout for anything suspicious.'

'Yeah, yeah, we know the drill. It's not as if it's the first time, after all.' I pause and consider my own comment. 'Huh, look at that — I'm getting used to having my life threatened. I wonder what that says about me.'

A long, martyred sigh comes from my right, and I turn to find Egan slowly shaking his head.

'What?' I ask him.

'You may find the situation exciting, dear,' he says, 'but I would much rather it didn't happen so often.'

Stenson chuckles before reaching for his notepad. He flips it open. 'I managed to find that nun you told me about.'

'Sister Anne?' I ask.

'Yes, she lives in a convent in Stratford, a few streets away from the church.'

'Did you talk to her yet?' I stand, excitement rising at the prospect of new information.

'It's my next stop.' He looks at me with a raised eyebrow and an expression I can only identify as inviting.

My excitement sags as I remember last night. 'I think your boss was pretty specific when he said I was to stay away from this case. He won't like it if you take us along.'

A lopsided grin appears on Stenson's lips. 'Sure, but if you two wanted to go out for some fresh air... say on the East side... what would be the harm in giving you a lift?'

Egan stands too. 'I would be much obliged. My partner has poor driving skills on icy streets.'

Stenson chuckles, and I reach for my coat and Egan's.

'Did you know,' I tell the detective, 'that by a happy coincidence, Egan and I happen to be acquainted with Sister Anne?'

The young man feigns surprise. 'Oh, are you now?'

I zip up my coat. 'Yes, we met briefly. I think it would be rude of us to be nearby and not stop by to say hello — don't you think, Ash?'

My partner takes a step closer to me, and his fingers close around my arm. 'Terribly rude.'

Stenson shrugs his shoulders. 'I guess I can't stop you two from being civilised.'

19

S hortly before midday, we reach the convent where Sister
Anne lives.

It's a bulky, old building, and it stands on a wide patch of
grass, surrounded by oak trees with a frozen pond to one side. Its
tiled roof is supported by large ochre columns, which give it a
timeless quality. An elderly nun is shovelling snow on the path,
and Stenson flashes his police badge at her. She doesn't seem
surprised to find we are looking for Sister Anne. I suppose she
must know about Dawn's murder.

She leads us to the rear of the building and leaves us
standing behind a plain wooden door adorned by a simple silver
crucifix.

Stenson knocks twice.

The door opens and reveals a surprised Sister Anne. She
recovers in a matter of seconds and waves us in with a polite
smile and an offer of tea.

As we enter, I discover we're in her bedroom. There's a bed

and a bedside table on one side, a small desk with a chair on the other. In the far corner, there is a miniature kitchen which comprises two cabinets, a sink and a single cooking plate.

Sister Anne drags the desk chair over to the bed and motions for us to sit on both before she steps into the kitchen area to put the kettle on.

Egan and I sit on the foot of the bed, and Stenson remains standing nearby, leaving the chair free for our hostess.

'Father Paul told me of last night's events,' Sister Anne says, handing each of us a cup. Her gaze lingers on the white bandage on the side of Stenson's head. 'Such dreadful events.'

'We had a thought, from the beginning of this case, Sister Anne, that the killer could be one of your parishioners,' Stenson begins.

'It was a wild guess, but it made sense,' I add. 'That's why we set out to watch the premises.'

'You set a watch,' surprise seems to catch the nun off guard, and her right hand flies up to the silver crucifix around her neck, 'on a church?'

'It's perfectly legal,' the sergeant says.

'I—I didn't mean...' Sister Anne blusters. 'Of course it is. I'm sure. But—but on a church?'

'Evil can wear many disguises, Sister Anne,' Egan says, 'even that of a God-fearing parishioner.'

'Of course, of course,' the old woman nods, letting go of her pendant.

'In this instance,' Stenson continues, 'it would seem to be that of a man with severe burns on his face. Average height, thin and often clad in black.'

The nun takes a fraction of a moment to think before saying, 'I have never seen such a man.'

'Are you sure? He does not have a face you could forget,' Stenson pushes.

'I am,' she replies firmly. 'I have not seen the man you described.'

'How often do you go to the church?' I ask her, setting my empty teacup on the floor for lack of a table.

The question seems to surprise her. 'Every day, of course.'

I frown. 'For mass?'

She nods. 'In the morning and in the evening. Sometimes I stay the whole day, to talk with parishioners or help with the running of the church.'

'Huh. That's a bit odd,' I say in my best playing dumb voice. 'I don't remember seeing you that much during my watch.'

There's a momentary flash of panic on the nun's face, but she quickly recovers. 'Surely you must be mistaken. I go there every day.' She licks her dry lips nervously. 'Maybe you didn't see me amongst all the other people.'

I smile at her and nod. 'That must be it. What with all the snow and the cold, there were just so many people coming in and out, I must have missed you.'

I turn to face Stenson, and find that his fake smile has turned somewhat predatory. 'Tell me, Matt, did you miss her too? Because of the evening crowd?'

He nods, his smile not letting up. 'Yeah, I must have.'

Sister Anne's hand flies up again, and her bony fingers are now white with strain around the small cross. 'The cold, yes,' she says with too much enthusiasm. 'I stayed at the convent for the last couple of days. I remember now. I wasn't feeling very well, and it was just too cold to go out.'

Egan slams his teacup down into its saucer, surprising us all. 'Stop lying, sister. It's a sin — or have you forgotten.'

The outburst, more than the accusation, startles the nun, and she recoils a little in her chair. 'I don't know wh—'

'Stop lying!' Egan says again with even more strength in his deep baritone.

I turn to face him, surprised myself by his behaviour. He sits next to me, his back straight, tight lines showing in his face. He turns to the nun with all the silent, unmoving intensity he's capable of.

'You feign surprise, and yet you sound nervous,' Egan says, his words crystal clear. He sounds detached, frosty and a touch... mighty. 'You pretend never to have seen this man, and yet he had a key to the front door. You offer to help us, and yet you withhold information from us.

'You are lying, Sister Anne,' Egan states, with a pause between each word to allow them to sink in deep. 'Tell me why? Why would you protect such a man, if a man at all he is?'

'I—I don't...' the nun stammers, her fingers clenching the crucifix hard. 'I—I have...'

I can feel Stenson tense nearby and adrenaline starts pumping through my veins. Yet Egan's features remain collectedly controlled. He sits, looming. His aura takes on a calm-before-the-storm quality, even more intimidating because of his stillness and intensity. It rattles even me, and I hold my breath for what is to come.

'If you mean to utter more lies, Sister Anne, I believe it

would be best for you to stop talking altogether,' Egan continues. He leans forward ever so slightly.

'I can hear them in your voice, you know — the lies,' he whispers, letting the last word hang in the air.

A small whimper escapes Sister Anne, and Egan moves back, resuming his former defiant posture.

'It is my gift,' he continues, his tone no longer that of confidence. It burns with its coldness. 'Bestowed upon me by our Lord. I *see* deceit in people's words — like the colours of a painting.'

The nun shrinks some more at Egan's words.

I chance a nervous glance towards Stenson and see that he is as uncomfortable and lost as I am. Yet he remains silent and unmoving, waiting to see how this exchange will play out.

'You were lying the day we met, and you are lying today,' Egan continues his baritone, clear in its eloquent quietness. 'You protect that man, that killer; tell me why, Sister Anne? Who is he to you? Why do you protect him; do you not know what he's done?'

The silence stretches after each of Egan's questions. The tension is so thick you could cut it with a knife.

'He's one of the children of our Lord,' the woman pleads in response. 'A lost lamb that must be brought back to the flock.'

At her admission, Stenson moves. In three quick strides, he positions himself behind the nun's chair and just in front of the wooden door, blocking the exit should she make an attempt to flee.

The religious woman seems too distraught to notice the sergeant's action or even the fact that she's just confessed to knowing a serial killer. All of her attention is directed at my partner.

'Enough!' Egan slams his cup in the saucer again, and I hear porcelain crack this time. 'He's not a lamb, and he's not lost. He lives in a world of darkness and of sin. He's a killer and a vicious one at that. Don't you know what he's done? Do you want me to tell you? Should I regale you with the gruesome details? Should I tell you about the red blood on their deathly, pale arms? Do you want me to describe the black nylon that pierced their fragile, milky-white flesh?'

'No, please. No. No more.' With tears in her eyes, Sister Anne brings up both hands to cover her ears as she violently shakes her head. 'No more, no more.'

Egan isn't finished. His regal voice covers the poor woman's pleas. 'Maybe I should tell you, Sister Anne, how he broke the pianist's fingers. Or would you, perhaps, like to hear how he killed sweet innocent Dawn? I'm sure you knew her. How many times did she sing for you? Well, after he killed her, he sewed her eyelids open. You could discuss that with her parents the next time you see them at mass.'

'He's lost!' Sister Anne cries out, her shaking voice topping Egan's for an instant.

That stops my partner.

'He's just lost,' Sister Anne continues. 'It's not his fault.'

The woman's tone is broken, a clear sign of defeat. We have her, and I feel Egan relax a fraction next to me. I reach for his hand, clasp my fingers around it. His fingers are balled up in tight fists, but they begin to relax at my touch.

'What's his name?' Stenson asks from his place in front of the door.

The beginning of a prayer passes the nun's lips.

'His name!' the sergeant asks again, louder.

'J—Joseph,' she stammers, holding onto the little cross hanging from her neck.

'Joseph who?'

'I don't know his last name. The boy was brought to us twenty years ago after a fire destroyed his home and killed his mother.'

The nun's shoulders sag, and her face takes on a distant, reminiscing look face as she continues, 'Our previous Mother Superior placed him in my care. I watched over him, tended to his wounds. The poor boy; he was in so much pain. I prayed for him, and eventually, his pain lessened.

'He was quiet, my Joseph. Always so quiet. But intelligent. There was a light in his eyes; a bright, bright light.' She lets go of the crucifix and starts to rock back and forth, apparently lost in her memories. 'He's one of the angels, *my* little angel. He's special; there's a design for him. God has a plan for each of his creatures.'

'What of the boy's father?' Stenson asks, clearly unnerved by her litany. His authoritative voice seems to bring the woman back to her senses.

Sister Anne blinks heavily twice. 'He doesn't come to the convent often. I've never seen him. He only comes at night. The Mother Superior was the only one who knew him. She said he was cold and distant, and he blamed Joseph for what happened. But it was just an accident. They were staying in a cabin, and Joseph was cold, so they lit up a fire in the hearth. A spark jumped out and landed on the rug; it caught fire.' She tsk-tsks.

'Joseph was such a young boy; how could he be held responsible?'

'Does his father know what's going on — what Joseph did to these girls?' Stenson asks.

'I doubt it,' the nun replies. 'He hadn't been here in a long time.'

'*Hadn't*,' I echo. 'You mean he's been back?'

'About a month ago, yes,' she nods. 'Joseph told me he visited him. I thought it was strange; he hadn't been here in years. He paid for Joseph's tutelage; he paid for our care... but that was the extent of that man's love for his child.'

'Paid for your silence, rather,' Egan slides in, in his customary cold tone.

'I loved him as my own,' Sister Anne replies, with passion. 'He's just lost; don't you see? The poor boy's been through so much.'

'Sister Anne,' Stenson cuts in before she can get into another rant. 'Where can we find him?'

'No. Oh, no!' She shakes her head violently. 'I won't say. I can't.'

Stenson's voice rises, and he takes a step closer to her. The floorboard creaks underneath him. 'Where?'

'Please, don't make me.' She grabs for her crucifix again. 'Please, Lord, give me strength.'

I step in, to try to reason with her. 'Sister Anne, there is a young girl with Joseph right now. Her name is Laurel Stubbs. She hasn't done anything wrong, but he's going to kill her anyway.

'Please, Sister Anne. There has been enough blood spilled. None of these girls deserved their fates — Laurel doesn't either.

You have to help us find Joseph and stop him before it's too late.'

The nun shakes her head again and tears spill from her eyes. The crucifix shakes between her joined hands.

It gives me an idea. 'That crucifix you're holding — you know what it stands for, what it represents? You know what He sacrificed. God wouldn't want Laurel to die — she's innocent. You have to protect her, Sister Anne, you know that. You know you cannot stand by and let her die. God wouldn't forgive you.'

'The cottage,' she mutters, almost inaudibly.

'What did you say?' I ask.

'The cottage,' she repeats, louder. 'In the woods, behind the convent. There's a small cottage; that's where Joseph lives.'

I nod to her. 'Thank you.'

The nun seems appalled by what she's just done. Latin words start to drift out of her lips in an uninterrupted flow.

'Someone will be with you shortly,' Stenson says, 'to bring you to New Scotland Yard. Please do not leave your room until then.'

She doesn't acknowledge him, as the prayers continue to pour out of her.

We close the door behind us and make our way outside again.

'Well,' I say, zipping up my coat, 'now we know who the mysterious "J" is.'

Stenson nods. 'I need to call this in.'

He phones his dispatch and asks for backup, while Egan and I head towards the small path that leads through the trees and away from the convent.

'We should wait for backup,' Stenson says, jogging up to us.

'There are three of us already, and we don't even know if he's here,' I counter.

Egan nods at that, and we continue to walk along the path.

'I'll take the lead; you two stay behind,' Stenson orders, walking past us in two long strides. 'At the first sign of trouble, I want you to run.'

I can't agree with that. 'And let you take all the heat? No way!'

The sergeant faces me, his expression serious. 'Yes, Alexandra, that is exactly what you'll do. If I tell you to get out, I need you to obey. I can't fight back and worry about your safety at the same time. I'll need to know that you two are safe, and won't risk getting caught in the crossfire.'

He has a valid point, and I nod my agreement.

With that settled, Stenson moves forward. It takes us less than five minutes to reach the cottage. We'd have been even faster if there hadn't been snow covering the path.

In a little clearing stands a small wooden cabin, thirty feet long maybe, and fifteen or so wide. It looks old and in dire need of a paint job, or at least some wood oil. It has windows on two sides, but thick drapes hide the inside from our prying eyes. No sound comes from inside, and I wonder if it's empty.

Stenson moves to the door and motions for us to stand a few paces away. I comply and take Egan with me to the spot Stenson has indicated.

The detective knocks on the front door three times. There's no answer.

'Maybe he isn't home,' I whisper.

Stenson knocks again, more urgently.

'Ash, can you hear anything?' I ask.

My partner leans in, listens for a full minute, then shakes his head. 'I don't hear anything.'

'Shall we go in?' I ask in a normal tone, no longer whispering.

'Not without a search warrant — I can't,' Stenson replies.

'Oh, come on. It'll take you hours to get one. Joseph might come back in the meantime, or he might kill Laurel. We can't waste time. Can't you pick the lock?' I ask.

He turns to me with empty hands, 'With what?'

I reach into one of my coat pockets and take out a small snap-over leather case. Taking a step forward, I open it, to reveal several lock-picking tools. It's an assortment of stainless-steel padlock and hook-lock picks. I bought the set on eBay from some dealer in China. Later, I spent a week watching tutorial videos and practising in my flat. I gave up after four fruitless days and decided to take classes with a real locksmith.

Bending down in front of the cabin's front door, I smile as I remember that encounter. The locksmith, a portly man named Benjamin, had thought I was kidding. His expression was quick to change when I handed him one of my business cards and several hundred pounds.

'Yep, it must be nice to be you,' I hear Stenson say behind my back. 'That would cost me my badge.'

With a chuckle, I get to work on the lock and have the door open in no time. I place the lock-pick set back in my pocket and, humming the first notes of *Bad to the Bone,* I take a diligent step to the side to let Stenson enter.

20

S tenson enters, a sure grip on his weapon, a handheld X26 taser. Egan and I wait outside until he steps back out.

'Safe,' he says. He takes cheap latex gloves out of one of his pockets, hands me a pair and one more for Egan.

'If anyone asks,' Stenson jerks his thumb towards the open door, '*this* never happened. It was already open.'

'I never saw anything,' Egan says, struggling to put on the tight gloves.

I chuckle at the words, and we enter the flat.

Joseph's place is a mess of pictures and pages torn out of what seems to be the bible.

'I don't think I have the words to describe this mess,' I tell Egan. 'The walls are covered in sheets of paper taped haphazardly and in a seemingly random order. Symbols and words have been painted over the documents: crosses and pentagrams, holy praises and the word 'Heaven' — painted over and over again in different colours.'

'Anything that could indicate where he's taken Laurel?' my partner asks.

I step closer to the wall. 'Not that I can see. *Porca vacca*, it's going to take hours to go over everything. The place is littered with loose sheets.'

I lean closer to one and start to read out loud, 'The angel said to me, "These words are trustworthy and true. The Lord, the God who inspires the prophets, sent his angel to show his servants the things that must soon take place."'

'There's something about angels here too,' Stenson says, a little further away. 'Matthew 13:41 — "The Son of man shall send forth his angels, and they shall gather out of his kingdom all things that offend, and them which do iniquity."'

I move to another part of the wall and find another verse on angels, this one circled in thick red marker. 'Does he think he's an angel or something?' I ask.

Stenson shrugs and moves further away.

'Sister Anne said something about angels, too,' Egan muses. 'That Joseph was her little angel.'

I shrug. 'Maybe that's where he got the idea.' I focus on the sigils and various crosses drawn on the papers. Most of them are unknown to me. I guess it'd take some theology expert to make sense of this mess.

'Here.' Stenson attracts our attention to another wall I have not yet seen, near the kitchen. 'The girls: all four of them.'

'There are photographs of each woman,' I describe, 'some taken in the streets, or while the girls were shopping. There's one of Dawn singing in the choir; one of Isabella dancing on a stage.' I keep looking at them and take in the various haircuts, the clothing to match different seasons. 'He had been stalking them for months.'

'How could no one notice him?' Egan asks.

'They must have been taken from a long distance. He was inside a car, or hiding in some bushes with a zoom lens, like paparazzi stalking celebrities.'

'I found some more.' Stenson motions for us to join him facing another wall.

I move next to him, and come face-to-face with images of women I'm unfamiliar with. 'His next victims... at least five more.'

'Any images of where he killed the first three girls?' Egan asks 'Or where he's holding Laurel?'

I look at the mess of documents around us, but nothing springs up. 'No; if it's here, I can't see it.'

'All right, we need to get a move on,' Stenson says in his professional-copper tone. 'Alexandra: go back to the living room, start on one side and keep moving forward. Scan everything: left to right. I'll start from this end.'

I nod and do as I'm told. Egan follows me to the living room and then drifts to a corner, mindful to stay out of my way.

I let my eyes linger one or two seconds on every document, then move on. I don't have the time to read everything, but try to take mental pictures of the lot. It's just like any other memory game: the more you practise, the better you get... and I have extensive experience.

Bible excerpt, symbol, bible excerpt, scribbles, symbol, scribble, bible excerpt. I finish the first wall, then move to the next. More bible excerpts, a poem on angels, symbols upon symbols, more bible excerpts. I move to another wall.

'Do you have anything?' I ask Stenson.

'No. It's just the girls. He has a lot of information on them: their schedules, their home addresses — but nothing regarding where they were killed.'

I continue to move along the wall, my eyes scanning over some more bible excerpts.

'Lexa?' Egan calls out to me.

I turn to face him, find he's moved to stand near the coffee table. 'What is it?'

He raises his hand, holding something for me to see, 'Is this a map?'

I reach him in two quick strides with a broad smile. 'Yes, it is. Where did you find it?'

'It was on the table.' He gives it to me, and I unfold it over the many documents that litter the coffee table. 'The type of paper, and the way it was folded, it reminded me of a City map.'

I discover that it is a map of Greater London, and I find East London. Sure enough, several markings have been made with a sharpie. I turn to Egan and kiss him on the cheek.

'Matthew,' I call out, 'Egan's found it.'

'Have I?' my partner demands, sounding surprised. The quick kiss also surprised him, I can tell. The tips of his fingers came up to brush his cheek, as if to make sure it really happened.

I look down at the map and easily find the locations where each girl was killed. 'Yes, you have. The only problem is that there are at least a dozen possible places where he could have taken Laurel.'

Stenson joins us, his cell phone in hand. He's pulled up his own map of London on it, and he compares it with Joseph's. 'It would have to do with music. Give me the addresses; I'll see what they match.'

'Building at the corner of Leman Street and the B126?' I say.

'Disused textile factory,' Stenson reads from his phone, after a minute or two. 'One of the potential victims appears to be a model; that place probably was for her.'

I continue to read out addresses, and the third one's the Charm — a former music hall, on Stepney Way.

I fold the map and place it in my bag. 'Let's go.'

We hurry back to Stenson's car. He's on the phone already, relaying the latest development to Langford and asking for a team to be dispatched to the address we found.

I reach for Egan's arm as we exit the building, intent on having a quick word with him before we set out for Stepney Way. He stops, while Stenson continues ahead.

'Are you all right?' I ask.

'Sure, why do you ask?'

'What happened in there...' I start, hesitantly, '...with Sister Anne, I mean. That wasn't like you.'

My friend remains silent, and I'm not sure how to continue. I'm not even sure I understand what happened. Did he really lose it? Or was it just a ploy; was he purposefully pushing the right buttons to make her talk?

In the end, I ask the only question that matters: 'Are you okay?'

I hear Stenson start the car; Egan does too.

'We should get going,' he says, in lieu of an answer.

'No.' I tighten my grip on his arm just a fraction, to let him know I mean it. 'I need an answer, Ash. Are you all right?'

I see him swallow and his lips quiver, for just an instant. 'I won't be until this case is over.'

I nod in understanding. 'You and me both.'

Stenson honks at us, and we join him, get in the car, and race off to find Laurel.

21

We are first on the scene, and we park by the kerb.

Twilight encompasses us, and the biting cold wind beats against our faces. We decide to enter the building without waiting for the cavalry to arrive — there isn't even a debate as to whether or not we should wait. If Laurel's in there, if she's being tortured at this very moment, then we're not going to wait another second before rescuing her. She's been in Joseph's grasp too long already.

Stenson draws out his taser again before creeping to the front door of the old music hall. The building is two storeys high, with huge windows on both sides of the front door. There is no light showing from them.

'Unlocked,' Stenson mutters, as he tries the handle.

He looks back at us before pushing the door open. Our gazes lock, and despite the darkness, I can read a silent plea in his eyes. I know what they're asking. He's silently saying, 'Promise me to run if I tell you to.'

I nod to him, slowly and deliberately, letting him know that I will. If it comes to it, I'll get Egan to safety... then I'll come back for Stenson's arse, but he doesn't need to know that.

Stenson turns back to face the building. He pushes the door open and enters. I follow at a small distance, with Egan right behind me. My partner follows me, with a hand on my shoulder, tension coursing through him.

'Do you hear anything?' I ask Egan, sotto voce.

'Mostly us, for the moment,' he replies.

We creep into the old building, displacing dust as we walk forward. The air is stale and lacks oxygen. I make an effort to move as silently as possible on the white stone floor. The inside of the building is even darker than the street outside, and I surmise the dust on the windows must be so thick it stops the last rays of the sun from entering. We cross a large lobby, and I see Stenson hesitate on which direction to take.

'Ash?' I whisper. 'Which way?'

'This way.' He points a finger to one side. 'Voices,' he murmurs.

Stenson follows the indication. He heads off to the left in the near darkness, soon coming to a stop near a swing door. I see feeble light filter through the keyhole.

Stenson goes in first. We remain in the lobby for ten long seconds, then we follow him.

The room is completely stripped, save for the remnants of balconies on both sides. All the rest has been ripped down to bare concrete. Dim light diffuses throughout the empty space. It comes from a single tiny bulb hanging from a loose wire, some-where high above us in the middle of the ceiling. It bathes the empty space in a weak, yellowish glow that makes it hard to discern anything.

My eyes adjust to the low light, and it takes me a second or two to notice a strange shape in one of the far corners. I blink several times until my vision adjusts, and I can make out the outlines of a human body.

It's a woman, gagged and bound to a metallic bar. 'Laurel,' I whisper, 'alive, and unharmed.' She's wearing the corduroy navy-blue pants and raspberry cotton wool jumper she was last seen in. Her blond hair hangs in a mess of curls and knots around her face. She looks uncomfortable, but sports no obvious injuries. It takes time, but she notices us and moans for help.

I have to fight the urge to rush to her. Instead, I take two more steps inside the room and come to stand near Stenson. Whatever words Egan heard in the lobby could not have come from Laurel's bound lips. One or more other people were here too. We had to be careful.

The detective has noticed Laurel's presence too, but he remains still, his taser in hand. He sweeps the surroundings for any possible threats.

I tensely follow his lead — my eyes try to look everywhere at once. I make a mental note of the door behind us, our escape route clear in my head. If only there were more light. We're now standing right underneath the light bulb, which diffuses a feeble circle of light around us, ten feet wide. Sadly, it leaves the corners of the large room in thick darkness. I'm not certain, but I think I can make out the outline of a closed door on the faraway side of the room.

Egan's fingers dig into my forearm, and I inch closer to him.

'We're not alone,' he whispers. 'I can hear someone breathing near.'

'Where?' I whisper back.

'Don't know, too weak to pinpoint.'

Blood turns to ice in my veins, and I wish I'd brought some kind of weapon with me. Even something as trivial as a crowbar would make me feel more comfortable than the emptiness between my clenched fingers.

Fighting to keep the panic at bay, I scan the darkness around us, only to find more black emptiness. The unwanted image of a man entirely clad in black creeps into my head as the hairs on the back of my neck stand up.

I try to catch Stenson's attention to let him know we're not alone, but he's half-turned away and facing the wrong direction. Fear of letting Joseph in on the fact we know of his presence stops me from calling out for the detective. Instead, I settle for waiting to be in his line of sight again, while I keep close to Egan.

Suddenly, a blur of motion has me whipping my head around towards Stenson's position.

A silhouette jumps from the darkness and onto Stenson, and I hear my friend let out a scream of pain. I take a step back, use one of my arms to push Egan behind me.

Stenson's taser clatters to the floor as the barrel of Joseph's weapon pushes against the side of his head.

'None of you move,' a voice wheezes, snake-like. 'Or I'll shoot.'

I freeze, and feel Egan go rigid behind my back.

Joseph stands shrouded in darkness, behind Stenson. They've moved to the edge of the light's reach, and I have a hard time making him out. He's clad in black from head to toe. He's shorter than my friend, and I can barely make him out behind Stenson's shoulder.

Only some of the pale flesh of Joseph's face is visible, underneath the brim of a dark hat. White, marred flesh. An eye with a mad look, no lashes and no eyebrows. The gloved fingers of one of his hands hold a gun to Stenson's head, while his other hand stops the young detective from attempting to free himself.

'You know what to do,' Stenson says as he fruitlessly tries to move.

'Shut up!' Joseph wheezes, reaffirming his hold on him and effectively pinning him in place. 'No one moves. No one speaks. I decide. *I* decide what happens.'

The sound of his voice creeps me out. It is too high-pitched to be normal — nasal, as if the man speaks with a broken nose. It also lacks strength, and I wonder if maybe his lungs were damaged by the fire too.

My gaze locks with Stenson's, and although his lips remain sealed, he manages to get the end of his request across. 'Run, Alexandra, save yourself,' his eyes plead with me. 'You promised me you'd run.'

'Drop your weapons,' the snake-like voice wheezes again. 'Now.'

'We don't have any. We're not policemen,' I reply, half-heartedly letting go of Egan to show my bare hands.

'But this one,' Joseph presses the barrel of his gun harder against Stenson's skull, 'is.'

I try to take a step forward, force my features to look relaxed and unthreatening. 'Please, Joseph.' Despite my efforts, my voice shakes. 'We only want Laurel. You're free to go. No one needs to get hurt.'

'No! No!' Joseph shouts. 'I decide. I decide.'

I freeze again, as the gun's barrel leaves Stenson's head to turn towards me. Super.

I raise the palms of my empty hands a little further, and concentrate on the unthreatening expression on my face. 'Okay, okay. You decide. You decide.'

The gun stays pointed at me, unwavering, unmoving. Everything could end in a second, I know. I hold my breath.

Stenson chooses this moment to try to free himself. He elbows Joseph in the ribs and moves to the side, in an attempt to get out of his reach. I duck to the side too, pulling Egan along with me as I move us out of the madman's line of fire.

For an instant, I lose sight of Stenson and Joseph, and when I turn to face them again, my friend is passed out on the floor. I curse as I notice one of his temples reddening under what undoubtedly was the impact of the gun's butt.

Joseph's weapon locks onto me again. 'Don't move!' he says. 'Don't move, or I shoot you.'

Joseph's features are easier to distinguish now that he's no longer hidden behind Stenson. His face displays uneven patches of pale white and red. He does not have any eyebrows or hair. His left ear looks like a chewed piece of meat, and his lips are thin, broken and the colour of blood.

I force myself not to avert my gaze, despite the flip-flop motion in my stomach at sight of him. With one hand, I grab the hem of Egan's coat and pull until I feel him stand right behind me, shielded from the gun by my own body.

'Why? Why do you want to stop me?' Joseph asks. 'Why do

you want to punish poor Joseph even when he has done nothing wrong?'

'We're not here to punish you, Joseph,' I say. 'Sister Anne sent us.'

Emotions are hard to read on the man's disfigured face, but he seems to perk up at the name. Stenson continues to lie limp at his feet. Forgotten.

'She's worried about you,' I keep going. 'She wants you to come home.'

'Sister Anne is kind to Joseph,' he nods. 'She's the one who told me of the angels.'

'She cares for you a great deal.' I force a smile to my lips. 'She's told us you are her angel.'

'Lies!' Joseph roars and the gun wavers dangerously in his hand. 'Lies, lies, lies.'

I'm taken aback by the outburst. Damn it, but this conversation was going well. I really have to put *How to Talk Down a Murderous Psycho 101* on next year's reading list.

'Lies!' Joseph bellows again. 'Filthy, ugly, disgusting lies. Bad taste, sour taste, vile taste.' He reaches a hand up to his mouth, wipes the back of his palm over it. 'Vile, vile, like the monsters who whisper in the night. Temptation; the devil's minions. Bless me, father, for I have sinned.'

He pauses, his eyes boring into me. 'Time flies; there is little left — leave us alone; the work is unfinished.'

'It's over,' I tell him sternly, trying for a new angle. 'We can't allow you to continue. Drop your weapon now!'

'It's not finished!' Joseph bellows before a violent cough hits him.

Tiny red droplets of blood fall to the floor, and I realise he's sick in more ways than one. 'You can't have Laurel,' I tell him.

The man looks at me, with his head angled to the side and an uncomprehending gaze directed straight at me.

I keep my tone strong, despite the fear coursing through me. 'It's over, Joseph. No more killing.'

'No.' The gun shakes in Joseph's hand. 'Father said you would come; he warned me. That's why he gave me this—' he jerks the gun from side to side, as a child would a toy, '— so you can't stop me.'

'God sent us, Joseph.' I speak the words slowly to make sure they sink in. '*He* sent us to end this.'

'You?' he spats. 'He would never have sent you. You are insignificant; father told me so.'

'And your father has always told you the truth, right?' Egan asks from behind me.

That halts Joseph in his rant.

Egan takes a step to the side, standing next to me again. It sends alarm bells ringing loud in my head. I turn a panicked look his way but, predictably, have no effect on him.

'Lies,' Joseph says again, but with less heat this time.

I return my attention to him, see the gun jerking in his hand. It seems he doesn't know which target to choose.

'He said it was your fault, but it wasn't,' Egan continues. 'God knows the truth, and so do we. He has seen your work; you've done enough, it can end now.'

'Father said it has to end too,' Joseph agrees. 'All I wanted was to know how?' he continues, with something akin to sadness. 'I wanted them to show me the way, but none of them would. Selfish bitches! They didn't even want to look at me; one even called me a monster. But I made them look. Oh, I made them look, and they saw.'

He coughs again, and more droplets of blood fall to the ground. Just as his hands start to shake, I notice he's paled even more.

'What way?' Egan asks.

'*The* way,' Joseph answers, without missing a beat, as if it is obvious what he is talking about.

'There is little time left,' Joseph says, turning to look at Laurel for an instant. 'She has to tell me how.'

'It's over, Joseph,' I say. 'Drop your weapon.'

'No!' His roar ends in a cough, but his shaking fingers are strong enough to aim the weapon straight at my chest. 'Father gave me this and told me what to do with it. End the game.'

The game... the words resound loud in my ears, as I realise we're still playing a game of chess. What is this then? Is Joseph a mere pawn standing on the path to the monarchs? What is the adversary's tactic?

'Your father controls many things, but he doesn't control your life,' Egan says. 'Not tonight.'

'No!' he shouts, and the weapon shakes violently again. 'Joseph ends the game, and the girl will tell me how to go to Heaven. Father said so.'

There is another burst of light and the loud bang of the weapon being discharged. I only have a fraction of a second to think. I hurl myself at Egan. I tackle him to the ground and feel a searing flash of pain strike my left arm.

'Die, die, die,' Joseph shouts, and more bullets fly through the darkness.

The shots are wild, incoherent. For a moment, I wonder if the man even realises we are no longer standing in front of him.

He keeps screaming and keeps firing until his gun clicks empty. He presses the trigger half a dozen more times.

Ignoring the pain shooting up my arm, I manage to get on all fours, and I lash out a vicious kick to his chin.

Joseph screams as he topples to the floor.

He's screaming, 'Die, die die!' as he hits the cold marble tiles. The gun jerks out of his fingers upon impact and tremors increase in the man's limbs until they turn into spasms that shake his entire frame.

The spasms continue, and things click into place in my head. The vile taste he mentioned; the blood; time running out... I scramble over to his fallen form.

'What did you do, Joseph? What did you take?' I ask, grabbing him by the lapel of his black coat.

It takes time for his attention to focus on me.

'What did you take?' I repeat the question.

'Only what father gave me,' he whispers. 'It won't be long, he said. It won't hurt, he said.' He coughs again, his scarred face contorting in obvious pain. 'He lied.'

'Who is he?' I hear Egan ask. 'His name, tell us his name.'

Another series of violent shakes course through the man's body again, and the black leather of his coat slips from my fingers.

'His name,' Egan asks again, louder. 'Give us his name.'

'Liar,' Joseph breathes out before his entire body goes limp. Blood trickles down the side of his mouth. His body convulses and shakes violently, once, twice and then it's over.

I lean down to check his pulse, but my fingers find none. 'He's dead. It's over.'

I hear Egan curse and turn to face him, surprised.

'Are you hurt?' I ask, heading back to where I left him.

I don't think he got hit by a bullet, but in the confusion I might have been wrong.

'I'm fine,' he says, and I give him a good once-over. He is crouched with one knee on the floor. He looks pissed off, but otherwise unharmed.

'You?' he asks.

The question reminds me that I got hurt, and I chance a look down at my injured arm. 'Got hit in the arm; it's not too bad though.'

My coat has a tear, and I can feel blood trickling down my arm, but I'm pretty sure I'll live to tell the tale. However, it is strange how thinking of an injury makes the pain double.

'Laurel?' Egan asks.

'Don't know,' I say, getting to my feet a little awkwardly. 'Wait here.'

I walk up to her, and she recoils in fear as she sees me approach.

'Whoa, it's all right,' I tell the young girl as I kneel in front of her. 'I'm with the police; you're safe. We're here to take you to your family. Everyone's worried about you.'

She looks at me with wide, pleading eyes, and I work the gag out of her mouth as gently as I can. She whispers a broken, raspy 'Thank you.'

'It's all right, Laurel. You'll be free in a minute,' I tell her. 'It's over. He won't hurt you anymore.'

It takes me some time to work the knots loose with one

hand, but I manage eventually. I help her get to her feet, and we head back to where I left Egan.

I find him next to Stenson. 'How is he?' I ask.

'Slowly coming around,' Egan says while kneading his fingers into Stenson's shoulder.

I let out a deep, relieved breath. I feel even more relieved when I hear Stenson moan. He blinks his eyes open a second later.

'The cavalry's here,' Egan says. True enough, a heartbeat or two later the sound of sirens registers in the distance.

By the time the first policemen enter, their torches dazzling, everyone is on their feet. Egan is supporting a slightly dazed Stenson, and I have a firm grip on a weak and shocked Laurel.

After Stenson flashes his badge at the constables, they help us outside. The crisp fresh air waiting outside is a relief.

Paramedics rush to us the minute we get outside, and they hesitate over who to attend to first. In the end, a blonde woman takes Laurel away while a tough-looking man sits Stenson down on the steps to shine a light in his eyes, despite the detective's protest that he's fine.

I'm whisked away towards an ambulance by a young, freckle-faced, ginger-haired man in his early twenties. Egan follows us, and within a minute, I find myself seated on a stretcher.

More police cars arrive as the paramedic helps me out of my coat. With all their blinking blue lights, they make the small empty street feel more like a dance floor than anything.

'Ouch,' I mutter as the young man's fingers prod at my bicep.

'Lexa?' Egan asks, concern loud in his tone.

I reach out a hand and grab his wrist. He twists his hand until he has our fingers locked together.

'You're lucky,' the paramedic says, and he continues his prodding.

I turn to face him, my eyes screaming bloody murder. 'I just got shot, man. In which world is that considered lucky?'

He blusters and says, 'I mean, this is just a graze. A good clean-up and a bandage will suffice.'

'Is it?' I ask, surprised. With the pain I felt, I was sure I had a bullet in me. Damn, what must that be like, then?

'Yep,' he says, reaching for a nearby bottle. 'Hold still — this might hurt.'

The kid pours something onto the wound, and then I *really* scream bloody murder.

22

Once I'm cleaned up and bandaged, I get to my feet and shrug my coat back on.

Amid the surrounding mayhem, it takes me some time to find Laurel. She's sitting on a stretcher with a heavy blanket around her shoulders.

DI Carrington is standing next to her, ensconced in a thick beige coat, and I'm not at all surprised to find her there. She still had a vested interest in this case, despite having had it taken away from her. The short, dark-skinned woman looks tired but pleased. She nods at me, over the distance, and I return the gesture.

She's gone by the time we make our way over to Laurel. From up close, I note that the young singer has regained some colour in her cheeks. She offers us a half-smile when she recognises us.

Langford makes his grand arrival as I'm about to ask Laurel how she feels. The DI fails to even acknowledge our presence.

'I've spoken with your parents,' he tells Laurel. 'They'll meet us at the hospital with your brother.'

'Thank you,' she murmurs, apparently unsure what to do with herself.

'Why, DI Langford,' I say with false cheer, 'it is a pleasure to see you've finally decided to turn up.'

His face, as he turns on me, is a comical mix of outrage, hate and that thing blowfish do when they keep opening and closing their mouths.

I can't resist torturing him some more. 'Anything else we can help you with tonight? Another serial killer to catch, maybe?'

I'm aware of the blonde paramedic saying that it's time she took Laurel to the hospital, but I keep my attention focused on Langford; the display of colour and emotions on his face is a rare treat.

'You,' he spits, waving a thick, gloved finger in my face. 'One of these days, I swear...'

'You're welcome,' I tell him with a regal smile.

He huffs and grumbles something inaudible before stomping off somewhere. He almost bumps into an oncoming Stenson as he does.

'Hey,' the sergeant says, coming to stand next to me. 'You guys okay?'

'I got shot,' I say. 'Egan's fine.'

'It's just a graze,' my partner says.

'That was caused by a bullet, thank you very much,' I add.

Stenson chuckles before directing his attention to Laurel being loaded into the ambulance.

'Are you all right, Ms Stubbs?' he asks. The woman nods,

and the paramedic jumps out of the back of the ambulance. Stenson raises a hand to stop her from closing the back door.

'One last question, Ms Stubbs,' Stenson says. 'That man's father, did you see him?'

'No,' she shakes her head. 'I was locked in another room when he came.'

'Could you hear them talk?' Egan asks.

'Not every word, but some.' Laurel scrunches up her brow. 'He wasn't pleased. He said his son had gone too far, brought too much attention to himself; that it had to end.'

'I'm sorry, but I have to take her to the hospital,' the blonde woman interrupts.

'Just one minute,' Stenson asks. 'It's important.'

'One minute,' she agrees, and we all turn our attention back to Laurel.

'I think he gave him something to take,' Laurel says.

'The poison,' I mutter.

'He was gone when the man brought me to the main room and asked me to sing for him.'

'Did he ever tell you why he chose you?' I ask her. 'What he wanted?'

She shudders. 'He said I was a godsend. He kept asking me for the way to Heaven.' Tears spring to the woman's eyes and her breathing quickens. 'I didn't know; I tried telling him, but he—he...'

'All right, that's enough.' The paramedic steps in. 'We're taking her to the hospital. You're welcome to question her there, once the doctor has cleared it.'

We all step back, and she closes the ambulance doors in our faces.

'I'm sure we'll soon have an ID on this Joseph,' Stenson says. 'It'll be my pleasure to arrest his father for being an accomplice. And for providing him with that gun,' he mutters.

'I wouldn't be so sure,' Egan says.

'What do you mean?' I ask.

'I bet you my favourite CD you'll never have his full name,' he says. 'The Sorter will make sure of that.'

'The Sorter?' Stenson says, bewildered. 'You're not still thinking he's involved?'

I snort bitterly. 'Who did you think the "us" in Joseph's warning note referred to? Damn it, this was another of the Sorter's games, and he was one move ahead of us all along.'

'Not you too, Alex,' Stenson says.

I turn to face Egan, grab his forearm. 'You figured it out earlier, didn't you? That's why you kept asking for his name.'

Egan nods.

'*Porca vacca*. It was a gambit,' I mutter.

'A what?' Stenson asks. 'What am I missing here?'

'A gambit. It's a chess term. It's when you willingly sacrifice a pawn to protect the king or the queen. The Sorter was in that building earlier. Joseph was his son.' My heart picks up at my own words. It was his son, and he died because of us. 'He poisoned him when he found out we had his location.'

'My phone call for backup,' Stenson says, understanding.

'He tried to protect Joseph for as long as he could, but once he realised the game was over, he sacrificed his own son to keep us from finding his true identity,' I add.

'We are nowhere closer to finding his true identity,' Egan says. 'And now that his son is dead, because of us...'

'There will be hell to pay for it,' I finish for him.

'We still have to search the music hall; there may be some evidence, and something that'll help us put a name on the man.' Stenson says. 'I'll double-check every result, and make sure no one is tampering with the evidence.'

'You need to be careful, Matthew,' I tell him. 'Don't trust anyone.'

He nods. 'I won't. You guys need to be on the lookout too. No more unnecessary risks and no high-profile cases for a while.'

I nod back to him, then step closer to Egan and offer him my arm.

'Goodnight, Matt,' I say with a goodbye smile.

He returns the smile, 'And to you.'

Egan and I step away from the blinking police cars and crowd of people barking orders at each other.

'Looks like we're on foot, partner,' I tell Egan, looking at the road ahead. The asphalt contrasts starkly against the white which covers the pavement.

'It's quite all right,' Egan replies. 'A bit of fresh air will do us good after...' he waves a hand in front of him.

I hum my agreement. 'I would like to make a stop on the way if you don't mind.'

As we start to walk to the nearest Tube station, I pull out my phone and call Mrs Doughton's number. She greets me with a voice that doesn't waver and sounds stronger than I've ever heard her before.

'I wanted to let you know we found him,' I tell her. 'The man who took your daughter.'

The news shocks her, and I hear her breath picking up. 'Have the police arrested him?' she asks, her voice shaking.

'No. He's dead. He won't hurt anyone ever again.'

Her contented sigh is unmistakable. 'That's good. Thank you for letting me know.'

'It's the least we could do.'

'Please extend my thanks and regards to your colleague,' she adds, before saying goodbye.

Egan, who heard everything, wisely remains silent as we keep walking. It is under a dark, starless sky that we make our way to West Ham cemetery.

I read in the papers that Isabella's funeral was held a week after her death. I thought about attending, but never found the courage to show up. It had not felt right to pay my respects while her killer was still at large. Today, it seemed fitting.

We bought some flowers on the way, from a late-night shop. I chose white roses because they reminded me of the ballet dancer.

'Do you know what my mother told me the other day?' I ask Egan, as the cemetery appears in the distance.

I answer my own question an instant later. 'That I'm solving crimes, one sleepless night at a time. Do you think she's right? Am I pushing myself too hard?'

'Do you think you are?' Egan asks.

'After we found Isabella, I couldn't help but think that one less coffee break, one less talk with Stenson would have got us there in time.'

'And what do you think now?' Egan asks as we enter the cemetery.

Images of Joseph's cottage spring back to mind at that. The notes on the wall, the victim's pictures. I have a whiteboard in my bedroom that often ends up covered in pictures and scribbles when I'm on a case. The comparison makes my insides coil.

'I've seen what zealotry can do to a person.' I swallow hard. 'I don't want this job to drive me mad.'

Egan's fingers leave my forearm, and his arm comes to rest around my shoulders an instant later, in a comforting half-embrace. 'Then don't let it.'

We walk the rest of the way in silence.

'Isabella Marie Doughton,' I read from the headstone. '1988-2012. Loving daughter and treasured friend.' The slab is dark-grey, and the text very light. 'There is also an engraving of a ballerina.'

Flowers already cover the dancer's grave. I crouch down and place a single white rose on the snow. Egan leaves his atop the headstone. Then, removing his glove, he runs down his fingers along the lines that form Isabella's name and the engraving below.

'I'm sorry we were too late, Isabella,' he says, his voice thick with emotions. 'May you rest in peace.'

23

The twenty-fourth of December dawns on us nine days later and surprises even me. With my head so wrapped around our latest case, I lost track of time. I'm at Egan's flat, helping him sort out his living room with the radio playing music in the background, when the anchor alludes to the date. Suddenly my mother's 'You know where I'll be' parting comment as we'd left the flat that morning makes a lot more sense to me.

Sure enough, she would be slaving away in the kitchen most of the day to prepare the traditional Christmas feast. We always celebrate the Italian way, and have our Christmas dinner on Christmas Eve. Coincidentally, it was a good thing that Egan and I found something to occupy ourselves and get out of her hair. I tried helping her out once or twice, but two Neve women in a kitchen is a recipe for a disaster.

As I finish re-hanging the curtain I had to take down so that the repairman could change the window, I wonder if Egan's realised today's date, or if he's as lost as I am calendar-wise.

My friend is rearranging his book collection. I offered to do it for him, but he was adamant political essays should not be placed next to medieval warfare, and philosophical master-pieces should not, under any circumstances, be placed next to whatever it was I tried to squeeze in after that thick leather-bound volume.

On the off-chance that my partner hasn't been paying atten-tion — and it's quite probable he hasn't, given how little he cares about the festive season — I keep my mouth shut about today's date and craft a plan to have him attend the supper without inviting him.

'Done!' he says, standing back up with a pleased look on his face.

'I'm about done as well,' I say as I finish taping the radio's power cord to the wall all the way to the power socket.

'Window's good, the curtain's back on. Your radio's working, and you won't break your neck because of the loose cable. Everything is now back in its place,' I announce giddily.

He raises a suspicious eyebrow at me.

'Okay, maybe not to the millimetre, but close enough,' I chuckle.

'Thanks for the help,' Egan says, hands in his pockets and a kind, relieved smile on his face. 'It's nice to be home again.'

I know he's missed the comfort of his sanctum, and his stay in my little flat with my mother and I with all our mess took its toll on him. He never complained, but I can see that's he's happy to be reunited with peace, quiet and order.

'How about you come for one last dinner at my place?' I say, trying for a cheerful yet casual tone.

Egan shakes his head. 'I think I've forced enough of my presence on you and your mother.'

'What? No! We were happy to have you around.' I try to be smart about it, look for a way that won't raise his suspicion. 'You haven't been home in what? A week? Is there anything edible left in your fridge anyway, huh?

'Come on, one last treat at *Casa Neve*. I'm pretty sure Mum's cooked for three already — we can't let that go to waste.'

A playful smile blooms on my friend's face. 'Well, considering you eat enough for two...'

I punch him in the shoulder, then hand him his coat.

He's still smiling as he shrugs it on.

———

The smell of food greets us on the stairs, and my mother singsongs a cheery 'Merry Christmas' as we enter. She's wearing a knitted jumper with reindeer on it. It's an old family thing she found in a storage box five or six years ago, which she insists on wearing every Christmas now.

We had a fire in our last flat, but of all the things we lost, somehow that ugly thing was one of the few stuff to survive. Fate's funny like that sometimes, I suppose.

'Christmas?' Egan echoes, standing poised on the threshold.

I grab his hand and drag him in. 'Yeah, you know that thing that happens once a year. Where you're supposed to gather with your family and loved ones and enjoy a good meal together. Us Italians celebrate on the night of the twenty-fourth of December. I told you that you were invited, didn't I?'

I close the door behind him and lock it for good measure. Egan's face tells me there will be retribution for this, but he's taking his coat off so I don't care. In my book, this is a win.

'Oh, mistletoe,' my mum coos, pink colouring her cheeks. I wonder how much eggnog she's already had before I realise she's pointing her finger right above us.

I look up and discover a darn branch hanging just above my and Egan's heads.

'She doesn't mean...?' Egan asks, turning bright red.

I look back down, catch my mother's eye and shake my head. Her smile turns frantic; it's a lost cause.

'Yeah, she does,' I say, taking half a step closer to Egan. 'It's sort of a tradition, you know.'

'Wait, wait,' my mum interrupts. 'Let me get my camera.'

She turns her back on us and dashes for her bedroom. *Porca vacca*, I knew I should never have got her that camera for her last birthday.

'Too late, Mum, you missed it,' I call out after her.

Egan chuckles next to me, a relieved expression on his face.

'Hold on, mister,' I say, reaching a hand up to cup his neck. 'You're not getting out of it that easily.'

'Lexa...' he starts.

'Hush,' I silence him, with a finger to his lips. 'There's something I wanted to tell you and now seems to be a good time.

'I know you're not close to your family anymore. I know you've spent so many Christmases alone you've forgotten what it's supposed to be like, but this year is going to be different.

You're not alone anymore; you're part of a new family now, and we're very happy to have you with us.'

I kiss him on the cheek. 'Merry Christmas, Ash.'

'And to you,' he murmurs before hugging me.

'Oh, I really did miss it, didn't I?' my mother says as we break apart. 'You'd better be quicker with the camera when Bob and I are standing under that thing.'

'I will be,' I promise. 'Where is he, by the way?'

'He should be here shortly.' She returns to the kitchen, and we follow her. 'Eggnog, anyone?'

My mother's boyfriend, Bob, shows up some ten minutes later. I introduce him to Egan, and he enquires about our latest case, which had finally made the papers.

"Dangerous serial killer caught by the Met," *The Sun* had published the day after Joseph died. It was apparently okay to let the masses in on the worrisome realities of life, so long as you brought them up in the past tense — what a joke.

Egan and I take turns telling Bob what we did. Of course, we skip over some details and keep the gruesome bits to a minimum. Bob, who works as an accountant, finds it all fascinating.

'Don't you encourage her, Bob,' my mother says. 'It's a dangerous job.'

'It's not.' I shake my head. 'She overdramatises things.'

'But you were shot,' she protests.

'It was just a graze,' Egan and I retort, at the same time.

The synchronised answer leads to a chortle of laughter all around the kitchen table.

Bob chuckles. 'So the killer's father, was he arrested?'

'Unfortunately, no,' Egan says, and I can tell he's choosing his words carefully. 'So far, the police have not been able to identify him.'

'They're still looking,' I add, also trying for elusive sincerity, 'but it seems they could not find Joseph in any of the government records, so his true identity remains a mystery. The people at the convent never knew his full name, and the money they got over the years for his care was always given to them in cash.'

I swallow down a large gulp of wine. In truth, a small handful of people know more about Joseph's father's identity. We know what he is, the master of shadows, a criminal matchmaker, a trickster — a skilled chess master who uses human beings as disposable pieces in his game. Yes, we know *what* he is, but alas... we don't know *who* he is.

The battle is not over — far from it. The pawns have been reset, and a new game is afoot.

EPILOGUE

The end of a year is a particular time. It calls for reflection. It's a moment where everyone looks back on what has been achieved, and speculates on what is yet to come. It's a time for wishful thinking and a time for regrets.

A year ago, at that exact same moment, I wasn't thinking about much. A year ago around this time, I must have been halfway through my second shot of tequila and trying hard to fit in at some posh party I'd been reluctantly dragged to. Irina had taken me there, of course. I'd never have gotten through the South Kensington mansion's front door otherwise. It had been my last night spent embracing the carefree attitude of youth.

When I close my eyes, I can still see Irina's blood congealing on the front steps of the university, a few days later. There are moments, such as tonight, when I cannot help but wonder if the choices that followed her death have been the right ones.

Did Mrs Doughton make a mistake when she hired us? Would hiring someone else have saved Isabella? Would another

PI, one who doesn't go out for drinks with DS Stenson, have made the connection between Dawn and Isabella?

Kohl pencil in hand, I sigh. I understand why people rarely take the time to reflect on their lives. Why once a year is enough. It's because there's nothing more annoying than questions which can only be answered by more questions.

Tip: It's best to keep that annual reflection time short.

'So, Lexa, dear, made some new friends this year?' I ask the woman facing me in the mirror.

The reflection nods in answer, between applying two brush-strokes of blush on her cheeks.

'Have you done any good deeds? Actions to be proud of?'

Another nod, less emphatic this time, because the hand applying the lipstick isn't a steady one.

'What about your plans for next year, then? Anything exciting coming up?'

The woman in the mirror remains quiet; she purses her lips — not in answer, simply to check her lipstick — and blinks long, mascara-coated lashes. She checks everything one last time with a critical eye. Only when she's as satisfied as she can hope to be does she allow her ruby lips to stretch into a shy smile, which should be answer enough.

There's no knowing when our next client will show up, and what the gig will be. Weeks can go by without anyone needing us and then, all of a sudden, nights of "hide-and-seek on the cheating spouse" will pile up.

In all likelihood, money will always be a sore subject to Egan and me. Still, I suppose if there ever should be a time to indulge in wishful thinking, it's New Year's.

'Sure, I've got plans,' I answer my own question out loud.

'Have you heard the phone shop below is closing? It would make a great PI office, don't you think?'

My smile grows as I realise we wouldn't even need to change our ad in the phonebook. Yeah, an office is definitely something to think about next year... but we're not there yet. Tonight is New Year's Eve, and I have a date with a cute brown-haired guy who has dimples when he smiles.

Stenson and I both marked it on our calendars and circled it twice in red. Neither will cancel, the date will not be aborted halfway, murders and other pressing cases will be ignored until next year, we promised. Tonight is the romantic dinner we've been talking about for the past three months. Tonight is the we-should-do-something-together-one-day we've been postponing time and again. Tonight is finally happening.

Tonight is a gastronomic dinner near the Thames. Tonight is the two of us holding hands and watching fireworks set the sky ablaze. Tonight is *the* night.

I put my hair up in an elegant ponytail and brush the loose strands until they lose their curl. They fall down in a cascade, their tips brushing the back of my classic cocktail dress. I move to stand near the door, ready for the evening to begin, and slip into my high heels. I look down at my watch... seven twenty-five; five minutes to go.

I should not be feeling this nervous. I could slap myself — if I wasn't too scared of ruining my make-up. There is no reason to feel like this, damn it. I'm not fifteen anymore. It's just a dinner...

'Oh, *porca vacca*,' I say to myself, looking down at my clothes — no, they're not clothes; I'm wearing a costume. This is not me. 'I should have worn something else.'

I skid back to the mirror and take a look. It is a nice dress, dark blue, and it flatters my figure. Is it too much though? It's too much; I should have worn jeans. Right? No?

I take quick strides back to the door, grab my coat and get out of the flat before I have time to change my mind again. I'm tempted to run down the stairs, but the heels force me to take the steps down at a steady, careful pace.

I am half expecting to find Stenson waiting next to his Volvo on the kerb, but the street is empty. I glance at my watch again: seven twenty-nine. He is not late... yet.

Butterflies flutter in my stomach as the anticipation grows. I keep seeing Stenson's face in my mind, his almond-shaped blue eyes; his tousled dark curls. I wonder if he'll have shaved for the occasion — I hope not; I like the three-day stubble.

The sound of steps coming from behind echo in the quiet night and I turn to face Stenson with a wide smile.

I hear the loud bang of a bullet being fired before I have the time to realise that the man facing me is not the detective I'd been expecting. The newcomer is too small, for one, too sturdy. Pain shoots through me, searing, blinding and mind-numbing. For a moment, it is impossible to think past it.

Then the world goes blurry, with dancing hues of indistinct lights. I feel my legs buckle beneath me. I'm half-aware of falling down and hitting the snow-covered pavement. Hard. The air is knocked out of my lungs upon impact and, despite my best efforts, I can't seem to be able to swallow it back in.

Blinking hard, fighting to keep my eyes open, I see snow turning red around me. Blood, I realise, my blood.

'Porca vacca,' I manage to stutter. 'Not just a graze this time.' And then the world fades to black.

NOTE FROM THE AUTHOR

Thanks for joining Neve & Egan's team!

If you loved this book and have a moment to spare, I would really appreciate a short review where you bought it. Your help in spreading the word is gratefully appreciated.

The story continues …

BLIND CHESS - BOOK 4

Professor-turned-PI Ashford Egan owes everything to Alexandra Neve. So when his kind-hearted colleague is shot and slips into a coma, he vows to take revenge. But even using every trick she taught him, a sightless investigator may be no match for London's most ruthless criminal kingpin.

Desperate to leave no stone unturned, Egan teams up with cops and criminals alike. But someone is hiding their true allegiance, and the professor fears he's being played for a pawn. With Neve's life hanging in the balance, Egan's terrified even Scotland Yard could be caught in a crooked game.

Can the cane-carrying private eye reveal a callous underworld and bring Neve justice before a deadly checkmate?

FURTHER READING
ALONE TOGETHER

They need all their wits to survive. But a language barrier could leave them dead in the water.

Anne-Marie Legrand is excited to begin her career as an au pair in Sweden. But when the young Swiss woman's flight from Geneva is struck by lightning, both the plane and her dreams come crashing down to Earth. Waking up bloodied and confused, she's terrified when she discovers the only other survivor is a middle-aged man muttering in a foreign tongue.

Scottish banker Killian Gordon may be a world traveler, but he knows next to nothing about wilderness survival. Stuck with a woman he can't understand, he struggles to take charge of the mismatched pair as they explore their surroundings. But the untamed land and endless sea surrounding them tells him no one will be coming to their rescue.

Focusing her efforts on building a sturdy shelter, Anne-Marie battles to keep morale alive with her disgruntled comrade. But with days on the island turning into weeks, Killian fears the odds of living through this nightmare are rapidly declining as the looming Scandinavian winter ensures a lonely and frozen death.

Will they face an even crueler fate than their fellow passengers?

Alone Together is a standalone survival novel. If you enjoy unlikely duos, dramatic landscapes, and adrenaline-fueled endurance, then you'll love Cristelle Comby's desperate tale of stamina and strength.

FURTHER READING

RED LIES

She's always followed orders. Now she wants out. The price of freedom may be her life.

Moscow, 1986. Soviet spy Sofiya Litvinova longs to end her days exclusively working sexpionage missions. But when she's dispatched to Stockholm to deploy her honey-trap tactics against a suspected Russian traitor, she has no choice but to comply. Until the assignment goes awry after the diplomat pegs her as KGB during the attempted seduction.

With her cover blown and life in danger, Sofiya agrees to help the man carry out his own covert mission while secretly reporting to her superiors. But when his dangerous blackmail agenda coincides with a devastating explosion in Chernobyl, her hopes for deliverance vanish in a cloud of radioactive dust and political powerplays.

Can Sofiya escape the agency's deadly clutches before she becomes expendable?

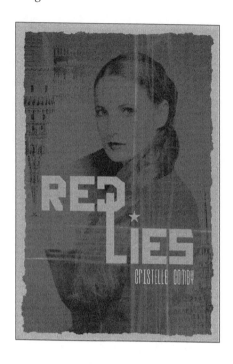

Red Lies is a fast-paced standalone espionage thriller. If you like international stakes, authentic historical details, and suspense with heart, then you'll love Cristelle Comby's captivating adventure.

FURTHER READING
VALE INVESTIGATION SERIES

Meet Bellamy Vale, a worn-out gumshoe trying to avert the apocalypse, one fight at a time...

PI Bellamy Vale's immortality is exhausting. Solving endless supernatural crimes may keep the bill collectors at bay, but the deal he made with a demon is taking a heavy toll on his mind.

Fighting back monsters from the underworld, booting out paranormal predators, and dodging dubious deities, Vale fears being able to interrogate the recently deceased wasn't worth the price of his soul. And as he doggedly attempts to do the devil's dirty work, the scrappy detective could find his ill-gotten powers aren't enough to save him from oblivion.

Can he dispatch the worst fiends of the darkness without triggering a universe-shattering nightmare?

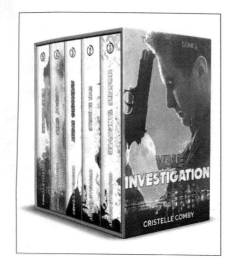

Vale Investigation - Box Set contains the wickedly rollicking five books in the Vale Investigation urban fantasy series. If you like sarcastic private eyes, magical mayhem, and noir-style humor, then you'll love Cristelle Comby's otherworldly collection.

ABOUT THE AUTHOR

Cristelle Comby was born and raised in the French-speaking area of Switzerland, on the shores of Lake Geneva, where she still resides.

She attributes to her origins her ever-peaceful nature and her undying love for chocolate. She has a passion for art, which also includes an interest in drawing and acting.

She is the author of the NEVE & EGAN CASES series, which features an unlikely duo of private detectives in London: Ashford Egan, a blind History professor, and Alexandra Neve, one of his students.

Currently, she is hard at work on her Urban Fantasy series VALE INVESTIGATION which chronicles the exploits of Death's only envoy on Earth, PI Bellamy Vale, in the fictitious town of Cold City, USA.

The first novel in the series, *Hostile Takeover*, won the 2019 Independent Press Award in the Urban Fantasy category.

KEEP IN TOUCH

You can sign up for Cristelle Comby's newsletter, with giveaways and the latest releases. This will also allow you to download two exclusives stories you cannot get anywhere else: *Redemption Road* (VALE INVESTIGATION prequel novella) and *Personal Favour* (NEVE & EGAN CASES prequel novella).

www.cristelle-comby.com/freebooks

Manufactured by Amazon.ca
Bolton, ON

43017710R00159